THE ERTH

THE WEARLE

ORCHARD BOOKS
Carmelite House
50 Victoria Embankment
London EC4Y 0DZ

First published in 2015 by Orchard Books

Hardback ISBN 978 1 40833 247 4
Paperback ISBN 978 1 40833 248 1

A CIP catalogue record for this book is available from the British Library.

1 3 5 7 9 8 6 4 2

Typeset in Goudy Old Style by Avon DataSet Ltd, Bidford-on-Avon, Wawickshire

Printed and bound in Great Britain by Clays Ltd, St Ives plc

The paper and board used in this book are made from wood
from responsible sources.

Orchard Books is an imprint of Hachette Children's Group,
and published by The Watts Publishing Group Limited,
an Hachette UK company.

www.hachette.co.uk

THE ERTH
DRAGONS

THE WEARLE

CHRIS D'LACEY

ORCHARD

For Christopher
The best present I can give

Character List

DRAGONS

GABRIAL: a young, good-natured dragon, just nine Ki:meran turns old, and referred to as a 'blue' because of his overall colour pattern. The biggest obstacle to Gabrial's development is his overabundant impulsiveness, which often frustrates his mentors and superiors.

GALARHADE: the Prime dragon, and a glorious red colour. He is two hundred and thirty-nine Ki:meran turns old when he takes command of the second Wearle to visit Erth.

GALLEN: commander of the feared wyng of fighting dragons called the Veng. Like all Veng, his colouring is an uninspiring, but unmistakeable bright green.

GARIFFRED: a blue wearling, born of Grystina. His choice of name is controversial, because it means 'flame of truth', implying he is closer to Godith than other dragons.

GARON: Gabrial's father.

GARRET: a talented mapper, thought to be the best in the Wearle.

GAYL: Grystina's female wearling and Gariffred's sibling.

GAZZ: a belligerent Veng.

GIVNAY: a greyish-coloured Elder, the spiritual leader of the Wearle. Rejecting the normal dragon life for one of meditative isolation, he is a powerful telepath and an expert in the art of i:maging.

GOODLE: the only other mature blue (besides Gabrial) in the colony.

(per) GORST: a mentor who teaches lessons in aerial combat among other things.

GOSSANA: an ageing and fearsome queen with an overinflated opinion of her rank. She has been sent to Erth to oversee Grystina's laying cycle. Dark green, with eyes that can change colour according to her moods.

GRAYMERE: a handsome purple dragon of the highly-intelligent De:allus class. He is a free-thinking scientist, interested in the natural geology of Erth.

GREFFAN: leader of the first Wearle to visit Erth.

GRENDEL: a young, beautiful female with touches of gold in her purple colouring. She is brought to Erth to assist Grystina during her laying cycle and beyond.

(per) GROGAN: an aged cousin of per Gorst and a long-standing friend of Gabrial's father. He mentors Gabrial as well as carrying out mapping duties.

GRUDER: a good-natured green roamer.

GRYMRIC: herbalist, potion-maker and a studious practitioner of the healing arts. His role is to gather up Erth's flora and fauna and assess the benefits of what he finds.

GRYNT: a tough, no-nonsense Elder with a streak of armoured silver on his throat and breast, which stand out against his overall light-purple colours. Grynt is responsible for the security of the Wearle and is the supreme commander of the Veng.

GRYSTINA: a mature female descended from the Astrian line, who claim to be able to trace their lineage closer to Godith than any other family of dragons. She has been sent to Erth to maintain the Wearle's breeding programme.

G'VARD: that rare thing, a white dragon. Huge, powerful and noble – a dragon that others respect and rally to.

THE HOM (THE KAAL TRIBE)

REN WHITEHAIR: a young lad of twelve winters who takes his name from his father, Ned, because both have hair lighter than the colour of corn. Ren is obsessed with skalers (dragons), a passion that frequently leads him into trouble.

NED WHITEHAIR: Ren's father. A brave but slightly reckless man. Like most of the tribe, Ned is filled with resentment about the skalers that have taken the Kaal's mountain territories.

MELL: Ren's mother. A gentle, free-spirited soul who can melt Ned's heart with her 'floating smile'.

OAK LONGARM: younger brother of Utal Longarm. A good bowman and skilful hunter. A man as sensible as his brother is foolish.

OLEG WIDEFOOT: so named because his feet, when together, do not point straight.

PINE ONETOOTH: a girl who has just one strong tooth in the middle of her mouth. Something of an enigma, Pine wafts around the settlement 'like a leaf on the breeze'.

TARGEN THE OLD: the aged leader of the Kaal, who rely on his wisdom to keep them on a spiritual path.

THE DREYAS: two women who look after the needs of Targen, especially during his 'journeys' to and from the Fathers.

THE FATHERS: the spirits of the (Kaal) dead.

UTAL LONGARM: the best hunter in the tribe, but an arrogant braggart.

VARL REDNOSE: a gruff, pitiless character who would do anything to serve his own ends.

WAYLEN TREADER: a farmer, and friend of Ned Whitehair and Oak Longarm.

ALSO:

GODITH: a female deity who, according to dragon legend, created the world from a single breath of flame and afterwards made dragons in Her i:mage.

GOYLES (or DARKEYES): dark, grotesque creatures with a remorseless taste for killing.

THE TREEMEN: a tribe who inhabit the Whispering Forest.

TYWYLL: a fabled black dragon allegedly lacking a third (spiritual) heart. Supposedly a fallen wearling of Godith.

WIND: Ned Whitehair's whinney.

Prologue

In the beginning was the sleeping dragon, Godith. And all around Her was a void that moved with Her gentle breathing.

For no reason known, at no time that could be measured, Godith opened her eyes and poured light into the void. And liking this, She chose to make an i:mage. A limitless universe in which She might live as many lives as She desired, within the bodies of countless dragons. She opened Her mouth and brought forth a great flame. Into this flame She spoke a word, *KI:MERA*, meaning 'place of fire and light'.

And when this was done, Godith looked upon Her i:mage and blinked Her eye. And from every sparkle that fell from that jewel came a creature or a mountain or an ocean or a forest. And many of those creatures were also dragons, made in the i:mage of Godith Herself. To each She gave a blessed gift, which was the right to speak the beginning of Her name whenever they spoke the beginning of theirs.

And so came Gawain, G'reth and more. And such was the power of Her jewelled light that other worlds formed beyond Ki:mera, some with creatures, some without. But nowhere else did dragons roam, until, as their wisdom and numbers grew, they came to understand that She was in the stars that blinked in the darkness around Ki:mera and that the stars were therefore as close to them as She was.

Knowing this, they i:maged openings in the void and reached into the darkness to explore every fragment of Her creation. Through their 'fire stars' they travelled, to colonise worlds beyond Ki:mera and awaken the glory of Godith across the universe. A journey that in due course brought them to a planet of plentiful water and diverse life forms.

When Greffan, Prime dragon of the visiting Wearle, commingled with the wisest forms on the planet, using his mind to look into theirs, he discovered that the creatures used the sound 'Erth' to describe their home. In the language of dragons this meant little more than 'dirt'. Yet even the dirt here was tingling with life.

Greffan communicated back to Ki:mera, describing 'Erth' as an unspoiled breeding ground for dragons. It was the last Ki:mera ever heard of him or of the twenty-three others in his Wearle.

This is the story of what happened to those dragons – and the dragons that came in search of them...

Part One

Gabriel

Part One

Gabrial

1

'Fold down your wings,' per Grogan said. He was huddled up almost in the shape of an egg, his words gruff and hard to hear against the wind. His gnarled old feet, missing the third claw on the left side, were barely visible beneath the curve of his chest. His scales lay taut against his aged sides, flattened down for warmth, less open to the wind. Yawning, he said, 'It might be nightfall before Grystina calls. You need to conserve your energy for battle. You're supposed to be presenting a measure of pride not hopping about like a giddy wearling. It will not look well if you fall off this mountain before you have the chance to raise your claws against G'vard.'

'I can't settle,' said Gabrial, letting the wind lift his wings to their maximum. His underwings, which were the colour of blue ice water, glinted in the frost-cooled sun. Across the valley, where the snow-capped mountains were arranged in a wave as blunt and uneven as per Grogan's teeth, G'vard would be waiting with his second, per Gorst. All that stood between them was a strip of fine cloud and this deep pool of air. Far below, safe in her birthing cave, the matrial dragon, Grystina, was curled around her hatching eggs. As soon as they broke she would call for a guardian to protect her young, a dragon to be her companion for life, a dragon that would have the right to call himself 'father'.

Gabrial was nine Ki:meran turns old, half the age of his powerful opponent. He was also a blue, technically a minor in dragon years, a turn or so away from the first blush of green that would earn him the status of roamer, a dragon free to fly where he chose. But the Wearle had known guardian blues before – most notably Gabrial's father, Garon, who had never quite lost the blue tints on his underwings and had always been classified by that colour.

When he thought about his father, Gabrial's wings did lower. Garon had been among the first Wearle of dragons to visit this planet, an expedition whose fate was still shrouded in mystery. For some reason, as yet undetermined, contact with them had ended abruptly. On the dragons' homeworld of Ki:mera, the Elders

20

had consulted and decided to send a second, larger party to investigate.

Among the sixty that arrived on Erth were mappers, healers, roamers, three Elders, two representatives of the intelligent class of dragons known as De:allus, and an entire wyng of fighting dragons called the Veng. The new Wearle immediately colonised a mountain range close to the open sea, just as their predecessors had. Three phases of the moon had passed, but they had found no trace of the missing dragons. And while the search for them was the highest priority that Gabrial and his companions faced, all other rituals were being observed – including the raising of young.

'Your impatience will be your undoing,' sighed Grogan. He belched and a curl of smoke rose from one nostril. 'The whole Wearle expects you to lose this contest. If you're happy to prove them right from the outset, then flap away and be done with it.'

'I'm not intending to lose,' said Gabrial, clawing slivers of grey shale loose from the ground on which he was perched. Such was the heat pouring off his body that most of the snow around him had melted, paring back the crisp white surface to its wet grey underbelly. 'Why are you here if you believe that I will?'

Per Grogan belched again. 'Tradition demands you

have a second for a fight like this. Someone has to see to it you don't make a fool of yourself. Rightly or wrongly, I promised your father before he left Ki:mera with the first Wearle that I would watch over you until your scales turned green – a reckless statement I might yet have cause to regret. What will be the most damaging, I wonder: following you here or the prospect of ridicule if this one-sided "contest" does not go well?'

'At least I put myself forward,' growled Gabrial, spitting orange-tipped embers around his feet. He watched a pair of roamers set down on a peak due east of him. Once Grystina gave her call, this entire ring of mountains would be filled with dragons, keen to observe the battle for her.

'And for that you have my respect,' said Grogan, tipping his grey head forward a little, 'but don't let this brief flirtation with glory puddle your brain. You're only here because the more eligible young dragons know what the outcome would be if *they* fought G'vard. They applaud you while blowing a snort of relief.'

Gabrial barrelled his chest. 'I courted Grystina and she did not reject me, therefore I have to fight for her. My father would be proud of me.'

'Your father was impetuous,' Grogan sighed, his scales clattering quietly as the wind got under them. 'A quality you seem to have inherited in plenty. But even he would accept it takes more than raw courage to defeat an opponent as powerful as this. G'vard will put your tail in a knot if you try to blaze your way past him. Stick to the tactics we devised and you'll hopefully survive with your wings unclipped. An honourable defeat is no shame, believe me. Put up a good display and the Elders might give you a wyng to command. Think of it as a training exercise, practice for the battle you *really* want to win.'

Gabrial tightened his eye ridges slightly. 'What do you mean?'

'Some matches are more appropriate than others,' muttered Grogan, looking across the valley for signs of movement. 'We both know your second heart beats for another.'

Gabrial gulped and ingested a wisp of smoke, passing it out through the spiracles that lined the sides of his neck. He stared into the open sky as if mesmerised by a drifting cloud. His soft blue eyes, yet to develop their jewelled state, barely moved as he thought about what Grogan had said.

Three females had come to Erth with this Wearle. One was Grystina. Another was the ageing queen, Gossana, a dragon so fearsome even the Veng avoided her. And then there was Grendel, the youngest of the three, whose primary role was to assist Grystina throughout her laying cycle and beyond. Whenever Gabrial thought about Grendel, the scales around his snout turned a deep shade of green. He couldn't hide the change in his colouring now.

Without looking at his charge, per Grogan said, 'I have seen the admiration you have for Grendel – and the regard she reserves for you.'

'Really?' Gabrial said, slipping forward as his feet danced on the wet rocks. 'You've spoken to her? She—?'

Before he could go on, a screech wound up from the pit of the valley, clawing at every fissure of rock along its way.

'That's Grystina. She's ready. Prepare yourself,' said Grogan.

'Yes,' said Gabrial, snapping to attention. It was true that his second heart ached for Grendel, but his primary heart was in control now, pumping great waves of energy through his body, heating his blood till the veins began to swell. He punched out his wings to steady himself, sending a snow cloud sideways over Grogan. By the time the flakes had settled, per Grogan had raised himself and the mountain tops were rumbling to the roars of dragons eager to see a fight. One roar carried above all others. It came from a distant peak

24

directly opposite Gabrial's perch.

'That's G'vard,' Grogan said. 'He lays claim to Grystina and demands you stand down. You must answer him.'

Gabrial knew this and was ready. For two days, since the Elders had accepted his challenge, he'd been training his throat to deliver the most powerful response it was capable of. Unlatching the bones at the base of his jaw, he clicked his mouth wide and called up a bellow which drove aside a wide cone of air and coloured the world every shade of orange. His fire reached into the valley in a jet half as long again as his body. There was a little more squeal to it than he would have liked and per Grogan was visibly displeased by the energy wasted in making a sound of such magnitude, but the effect was just what Gabrial had wanted. All around the mountain tops the air was popping with similar bursts of colour. The watching dragons were becoming excited. Perhaps the battle for Grystina would not be as one-sided as the odds suggested?

G'vard called again, strength and purpose pouring out of his lungs.

'Now you've angered him,' sighed Grogan. 'That's not a good start. And it won't impress the Elders either.' He swivelled his eyes toward the peak of the mountain the dragons called Skytouch where the silhouettes of the Prime dragon, Galarhade, and the other two Elders had appeared. 'This is not a fight to the death, remember? Produce a flame like that in battle and Galarhade will kill you if G'vard doesn't. All you're aiming to do is take a scale, not turn him to ash. Are you clear about the rules?'

Gabrial nodded. 'I can flame and claw, but not stab or bite. Eyes and hearts must always be avoided.'

'Good. What else?'

'No phasing.'

'None whatsoever,' said Grogan. 'Any movements through time, no matter how minor, will be seen as cheating. You'll be back in Ki:mera before you can scrape your last meal off your teeth if Galarhade detects a change in the continuum. What else?'

A second call went up from Grystina, the final call to battle. The assembled dragons burned the air in acknowledgement. All along the skyline now, more were arriving like a flock of giant birds. G'vard threw out another fierce roar.

'What *else?*' per Grogan repeated harshly, lashing his tail across Gabrial's chest to prevent the young dragon from launching too soon.

Gabrial roiled his wings in frustration. 'Only one i:mage.'

26

Per Grogan nodded. 'One. Don't waste it.' He pulled his tail away and Gabrial launched. 'Stay low!' the old dragon bellowed, adding to himself, 'The less far you have to fall, the easier it will be to stand up tomorrow…' And then he took to the rock that Gabrial had vacated and bellowed to per Gorst that his charge was in the air.

Likewise, per Gorst let it be known that G'vard had launched.

Two dragons, one theatre of air.

The battle for Grystina had begun.

2

Gabrial arrowed downward into the cloud, rolling once before levelling out and streaming with it toward the far mountains. He was following per Grogan's advice to fly fast below the layers and tease the white dragon with glimpses of him, before disappearing at the point of a strike. On a day as bright as this, blues enjoyed the natural advantage of being able to lose themselves in the sky. It mattered that the angle of the sun was right, but for a brief and sometimes telling moment Gabrial knew he could effectively vanish. And a moment was all it took, at speed, to lash out and rip away a dragon's scale. The first to deliver an opponent's scale to Prime Galarhade would be Grystina's champion.

But G'vard was a dragon of no mean stealth, and his second, per Gorst, was a clever tactician. Between them, they'd concocted an unusual strategy, which also made use of the cloud. Gabrial's first inkling of it came when it started to rain. He was confused, and rightly so. There had been no rain in the sky all morning and the cloud was too fine to produce the sort of wash spitting over his wings. Yet the droplets were definitely coming. Suddenly G'vard loomed up behind a semi-transparent wall of water and Gabrial realised what was happening. The white dragon was using bursts of *cold flame* to condense the cloud and drive the water across Gabrial's flightpath. As Gabrial splashed into it, four huge claws punched through the torrent. Their sharp tips closed like a deadly flower, grazing the small scales under his jaw. A moment later, his lungs were almost turned to stone as the thwack of G'vard's enormous tail fell across his breast. No scales worked loose, but the hit sent Gabrial spinning sideways. Every spiracle hissed in complaint. His fire sacs stuttered and temporarily went out. Dazed, he fell in a plummeting spiral. The gasp from the onlooking dragons suggested they feared for the young blue's life. It would have been a simple matter at this point for G'vard to swoop down and flick a scale off Gabrial's back or shear away the isoscele at the tip of his tail. (What humiliation *that* would have been: a sore stump instead of a sharp triangle.) Instead, the white swung round and waited for Gabrial to right himself, prepared to intervene if necessary and save his opponent from a fatal crash. For as per Grogan had rightly said, this was a test of worthiness, not a battle to the death. The Wearle could ill afford to lose any dragons.

After a drop that measured some thirty wingspans, Gabrial recovered. His fire reignited and his ear stigs rattled out a fierce alarm: if he didn't lift his head and do something with his wings he was destined to become a permanent feature of the valley floor. He heard roars of relief as he rolled three times and found the strength to enter a glide. It wasn't enough to prevent him hitting an escarpment and tumbling even further down the valley, gathering snow like a falling seed. Any sensible dragon might have accepted defeat. But Gabrial wasn't ready for surrender. He was stunned and pained all over his body, but the hurt had merely sharpened his senses. He flipped himself upright, roared for good measure, shook off the snow and looked around for G'vard.

The white dragon had landed behind him. G'vard had risen to his full height, just over a flame's length away. His jaws were open, his multiple, hooked incisors glistening and sharp against the smoke-stained pink of his mouth. It was a posture that would have made most dragons cower, and a ripple of fear ran through the blue now. When dragons grappled on the ground, rarely did the smaller beast triumph. Gabrial was strong, of good weight for his age, but G'vard was huge in comparison; the hardened veins in his formidable wings were almost as thick as Gabrial's front legs. But it was the eyes that Gabrial knew he must avoid. G'vard was fully jewelled and an expert in *glamouring*, the ability to mesmerise opponents with a stare. Yet it was a subtle glance at the eyes that saved the blue dragon and prolonged the fight. Something wasn't right with them. The eyes were shaped like jewels, with many angled sides, but they weren't glittering. That could only mean they weren't *real*. Gabrial was looking at an i:mage.

Of the many gifts dragons possessed, the ability to i:mage was the most prized – simply because the technique was so difficult to master. As early as the wearling stage, young dragons were encouraged to make structures outside their heads of the shapes they created inside them. These 'floating pictures', as they were sometimes called, had no substance and dissolved as the dragon's concentration wavered. Gabrial could still recall many of the 'blobs' he'd produced as a wearling. He had struggled in his youth to make anything worthwhile (his mother had called his first creations 'disturbingly different'), but had steadily improved with his father's guidance until he could make convincing i:mages that looked so perfect they had to be prodded to determine whether they were real or not. That was exactly what G'vard had done here, used his ability to create a duplicate i:mage of himself, even drawing some snow into the structure to give it depth. Gabrial took a chance and flew straight at it. The fake G'vard exploded in a burst of snow, hiding the blue just long enough to avoid the swing of real claws concealed behind the i:mage. Once again, G'vard was left frustrated and the young contender escaped.

And now Gabrial had a minor advantage. G'vard had used up his chance to i:mage. If he tried again he would be disqualified and the contest would default to Gabrial. What's more, Gabrial was in the air again, where he was more at ease. On a straight flight, G'vard would have left him behind in five wingbeats. But in aerial combat, Gabrial was easily more agile, and he proved it several times in the next few clashes. Twice the white dragon closed on him at speed, and twice Gabrial deftly swooped away. At one point, he cleverly folded his wings and darted between the white's stout legs, almost nicking a scale from his belly. The watching dragons hurred in appreciation. The blue was proving an entertaining adversary. Was it possible he could actually *win*?

Gabrial believed he could. But he was also aware that if the aerial exchanges continued for too long he was going to tire. One sloppy wingbeat, one miscalculated roll, and G'vard would have him. And so he moved into his final stage, which was to use *his* right to i:mage. First, it involved a little deceit. He swung toward G'vard again, apparently attempting to loop around him. This was a dangerous strategy. Halfway through the manoeuvre, G'vard twisted and caught hold of Gabrial's leg (the unscaled part between the knee and the foot), almost dragging the youngster to him. It was a terrifying moment, echoed in the gasps from the mountain tops. Yet somehow Gabrial wriggled free, banking away toward the only volcanic peak in the range – the open crater of the mount they called Vargos.

G'vard roared and gave chase. The watchers rumbled, thinking the blue was fleeing. But this was all part of Gabrial's deceit. He had saved enough energy to put a decent space between himself and the white. And as he flew over Vargos, in his wake he created his i:mage, a huge eruption of volcanic splinters – fire, hot embers, fizzling rock, spits of lava, dense black smoke. It took a huge amount of mental energy. Indeed, as he landed on the far side of the crater and turned to look for his pursuer, he almost toppled into the fearsome caldera his mind had created. The eruption looked incredibly real. It was almost as if the thrill of battle had strengthened his i:mage and shaken the entire mountain awake. Deep in its belly, it was grumbling worse than per Grogan at sleep. Gabrial thought he heard the sound of splitting rock, but ignored it as he set himself, ready for G'vard. He was hoping the white would come through the i:mage with his eyes closed – as he would if shielding himself from real sparks. Then Gabrial could pounce, steal a scale and win. But G'vard was nowhere to be seen. And the mountain was growling like a thing possessed. Out of it came a dreadful cry – a cry that sent a shiver running right through Gabrial. It was Grystina, calling to say she was in danger. She was birthing in this mountain, Gabrial realised. She was *here*, in the caves of Vargos.

In two wingbeats he had crossed the crater to the other side, though it might have been better for him to sink into that hole and never come out. What he saw as his i:mage dispersed struck a chord of terror in all three of his hearts. Dragons were descending from the mountain tops, swooping on an area halfway down Vargos, coming away with great lumps of stone. G'vard was among them. So too, per Gorst. A whole section of the slope had collapsed, in a slurry of rocks and churned-up snow.

With a flap of wings, per Grogan landed beside Gabrial.

'W-what happened?' Gabrial stuttered, blinking in shock.

'What were you *thinking*?' per Grogan hissed, steam emerging through the gaps in his teeth. His eyes held a deeply troubled look.

Gabrial was shaking. What *had* he been thinking? Embers. Smoke. A distraction, nothing more. Not this. Not a landslide. That just wasn't possible.

'The mountain cracked,' per Grogan said, as if he'd like to pick it up and drop it on Gabrial's foolish head. 'Did you i:mage a solid rock fall?'

'No,' said the startled blue. 'I…I can't do that, you know I can't.' He looked at the frantic activity below. The whole Wearle, directed by an Elder called Grynt, was trying to free a passage through to Grystina and her precious wearlings. Gabrial shook his head in horror. 'We have to go and help.' He put out his wings.

'No,' said Grogan.

Gabrial looked into the old dragon's face. Lines were creasing around Grogan's eyes. 'But—?'

'They may turn on you, Gabrial. Godith have mercy, it would be better if you fled.'

'But I didn't *do* anything,' Gabrial repeated. 'I can't

35

i:mage physical effects.'

Per Grogan fanged his lip. 'That's not the way the Veng will see it.'

Gabrial tightened his claws, sending a small stone tumbling down the mountainside. Grogan was right; if the Veng set upon him they would rip him to pieces and ask questions later. But his fate truly rested on the judgment of the Elders. 'I'm innocent,' he said. 'I have nothing to fear. We must aid Grystina. If we fly into the crater we might be able to reach her from the in—'

'No!' Again, Grogan held him back. 'Look at me, Gabrial.' He dug his claws into the young dragon's chest. 'She's already dead. She couldn't survive a rock fall like that. You wouldn't get through the melt pools anyway.'

Dead? The word felt like a stone on Gabrial's tongue. Dead? He had killed a potential *queen*? And almost certainly her wearlings too. Wearlings that could have been his to care for. His knees gave way and he sank to his haunches, a sickness as ferocious as any eruption beginning to bubble up deep in his gut. As if his nerves weren't strained enough, faint cries began to ripple the air. The excavating dragons had found something.

Gabrial and Grogan looked down together, in time to see G'vard, blackened by dirt, presenting a moving bundle to the prime dragon, Galarhade. It looked like a wearling. It *was* a wearling. A female. A *wearmyss*. The whole world fell silent for it. For a moment, the entire planet was still. All that moved were the feet and tail of that baby dragon, reaching out for her absent mother. Galarhade tilted his head very slightly. He grunted something which sounded like a question. G'vard shook his head from side to side. The onlooking dragons all lowered their gaze. A wave of sorrow flowed up the mountain and all but stopped poor Gabrial's hearts. He knew what that head shake meant.

Grystina, as per Grogan had suspected, was dead.

3

The Elders called the Wearle to gather at Skytouch, where the mountain flattened out at the bottom of the waterfall and the water spread forth like a seeping wound to form a restless lake, always on the verge of freezing – or thawing. The result was a conflict of shuffling ice that flowed over the basin at its farthest edge into any number of smaller cascades, before joining the permanent glacial lane that surged between the mountains in snow-thickened layers to the open sea. On their homeworld of Ki:mera, centuries of flamework had led to the carving of ornate settles at meeting places just like this. Here, the dragons perched wherever they could, mainly clawing to ledges on the lower mountainside. Gabrial sat some ten strides from the water, an uncomfortable figure on an even more uncomfortable seam of boulders, guarded at his rear by two of the Veng who had forcefully escorted him there. On the shoreline in front of him lay the tragic figure of Grystina, stone chips in the traps of her scales, rock dust blighting the pleasing gradations of her mid-green body. Just beyond her, at the near-centre of the lake, on a natural stone pillar that poked through the ice field like a discarded tooth, sat the Elders, Grynt and Givnay, between them the imposing figure of the Prime dragon, Galarhade.

Galarhade was old. It showed in the furrows around his eyes and in the hairs which grew unflatteringly long from the base of his jaw. These days, his tail rarely stood straight, but lay curled around his creaking legs (to warm the failing joints, some said). His breast, once as bright as the fresh ice around him, was slowly losing colour, the first indication that death's scale had set forth to shadow his eyes. But these were minor imperfections. Through most of his body, including his wings, he was still a magnificent red – a colour not given to a dragon at birth but a prize earned from a dance with longevity. Green or purple was the base colour of most dragons, who grew into it (from blue) around their ninth turn. They would keep that shade for the rest of their lives – unless they lived to be Galarhade's age. Then the scales would cease to renew but at the same time gradually convert to red, like a tree observing the onset of winter. Unusually, for one so aged, Galarhade had lost none of the glistening highlights on his eyes or wings, most notably along the run of fine scales which protected the bony edges of the wing. Too many 'lytes' (scales which sparkled) were generally considered unappealing, though dragons had argued for and against this feature for centuries. Decorative braids on the face or zig-zagging accents along the neck were the trimmings that determined beauty in females or handsomeness in males. The debate went on. Many believed that Galarhade possessed the perfect mix: enough lytes to make his contours shine, plus the finest example of gradation ever seen, those sweeping tints across the underwings and chest that truly determined a dragon's 'look' and set one dragon apart from another. The tail was also a source of great vanity. Those creatures blessed with an elongated hue that flowed from their neck right through to the isoscele were much admired among their peers. G'vard, for instance, despite being white, and therefore one of the genetic minority that had hatched outside of the standard pattern, possessed an enviable range of near-white tints that almost touched yellow at his isoscele (a colour much desired, but rarely seen). G'vard was tipped to be an Elder someday. But for now, the wisdom and majesty of Prime Galarhade was the voice that prevailed upon the Wearle.

He summoned G'vard to stand beside the blue. It was the closest they had come since the battle terminated.

'Is there no hope?' the Prime dragon said. He had spoken softly, but his words rolled across the lake with such stark gravity that even the clattering ice fell silent.

'None,' said G'vard. 'Grystina was dead when we found her.'

'That is not what Prime Galarhade meant,' said Grynt, the fearsome-looking Elder at Galarhade's right.

Galarhade raised a single claw, enough to keep Grynt in his place. 'What of the drake?' He meant the male wearling. A mother would only ever lay two eggs: one male, one female.

G'vard hesitated. His white chest rose. 'Missing.'

'Missing?' gasped Gabrial, blowing up a whisk of snow. He looked at G'vard. There was a faint speck of light in the white dragon's eyes, as distant as a pale Ki:meran moon. He was mourning the loss of Grystina more than anyone.

'Be silent,' said the Prime, barely raising his voice.

Gabrial bowed his head. He should not have spoken

41

out of turn, he knew, but he'd done no more than echo the rumblings on the slopes behind him. 'Missing,' G'vard had said. That meant there was a chance the drake was alive.

'When we entered the chamber,' G'vard announced, his words floating off his tongue like a fog, 'we found the wearmyss shielded by the queen's tail.'

A fresh wave of murmurs descended. Strictly by law, Grystina should not have been declared a queen until she emerged from the cave with her young, but no dragon was going to challenge the sentiment.

'Continue,' said Galarhade, waving for quiet. His ears, like his legs, were no longer at their best.

G'vard drew breath. 'The floor of the chamber had partially collapsed. Grystina had been taken into the void. All but the thickest part of her tail was buried by rocks that had fallen onto her. When we pulled her out, we raked away what we could of the rubble. We dug where it was safe to, but the debris was deep and so hard-packed it was difficult to clear. We believe it consumed the drake, because we could not scent him or find evidence of his body. One so young could not have survived such a weight of rock. His fire belongs to Godith now.'

'Have you looked for tunnels?' a sharp voice said.

Gallen, leader of the Veng, arched his body forward. He was on a ledge not far above Gabrial's right ear, a worrisome speck on the edge of the blue's vision. It was a general truth that dragons feared nothing except themselves, but if there was one class they cared not to cross, it was the Veng. Like G'vard, the Veng also differed from the standard colour pattern. They were bright green, almost emerald, not easy on the eye. They were often considered to be physically small, an illusion caused by their lack of gradation and the slender design of their bodies (they were sometimes called *sier pents*, a derogatory term that meant 'green fish'). There were no illusions about their power, however. One only had to look at their ferocious horns or count the battle stigs rising from the backs of their heads to know how intimidating they could be, even to a dragon like G'vard.

'Of course we looked for tunnels,' G'vard said. 'We found many fissures in the walls of the chamber, but nothing that resonated deeply when we called. And we have heard no cries from the drake. The roamers have been searching the outer slopes, melting back the snow, looking for openings. They found one unmapped cleft that may have a passage into the mountain – too small for any dragon to crawl through, though a wearling might crawl out. We dare not widen it lest the rocks collapse again.'

'May I ask a question?' another voice said.

Prime Galarhade's gaze swept up the mountainside, where a purple dragon with large yellow eyes sat beside a similar-looking one. 'De:allus Graymere will speak,' said Galarhade.

Graymere shuffled forward slightly. 'This may be of little significance, but it took a few moments for the rocks to fall, and Grystina had time to call out before the tragedy occurred.'

Gallen sighed and flicked out his talons. 'Get on with it, De:allus. My scales will have dropped by the time you've made your point.' The Veng had little tolerance for dragons that spent most of their time *prodding* things to see how they worked.

'My point is,' Graymere said with a growl. 'Why would she place only *one* of her wearlings in her tail for safety?'

That started a rumble, most of it scathing. The weight of many scowls bore down on Graymere, but when Gabrial looked across the lake he saw a thoughtful glint in the Prime dragon's eyes. Elder Givnay, he noticed, was paying particularly close attention to the words of the De:allus.

G'vard was less impressed. He raked the ground in frustration, making Gabrial jump. 'What does this matter? The deed is done. There could be any number of reasons Grystina failed to protect the drake.'

'But when I was a drake, I hardly ever left my mother's tail,' said Gabrial.

G'vard curled his claws into the loose grey rocks, almost grinding the smaller stones to dust. 'That's probably because you were as pathetic then as you are n—'

'Enough,' said Galarhade, ending the argument. He glared at G'vard, who lowered his head. For a moment, the only sound was the honking of birds as they flew across the lake. The wind snapped and changed direction. Snowflakes drummed Grystina's corpse. Galarhade shifted his position slightly.

'The words of the De:allus are noted,' he said, throwing his voice high up into the mountains. 'We may never know what happened in the cave. Let it simply be recorded that Grystina gave her life saving one of her young, perhaps choosing the wearmyss over the drake to foster the future growth of the Wearle.' He levelled his gaze at Gabrial again. 'Now we must examine why this tragedy happened and what is to be done with those involved.'

A stony beat rang out around the mountains as dragons pounded their tails against the rocks.

'Prime, I'm innocent,' Gabrial protested, his wing bones rattling in fear. 'Why would I want to harm Grystina? I fought for the right to protect her young. My i:mage was clear. I pictured embers in my mind, nothing more.'

This was too much for G'vard. With a roar that almost burst Gabrial's ear pipes, he turned on the blue and wrestled him, neck first, to the ground. He was quickly surrounded by Gallen and the Veng, summoned by Grynt to stop the violence. It took a vicious swipe from Gallen's left claw to claim the white's full attention. When G'vard looked up, one of his scales was hanging loose off Gallen's talons. A cruel jibe, perhaps intended to say, 'If you'd done this earlier, we'd have had another drake to protect the Wearle.' The stand-off that followed was brutally loud (though thankfully not physical). It took a huge burst of fire from Galarhade to calm Gallen and the white dragon down. The exertions left the Prime visibly weary. He had to breathe deeply to recover. He flapped Gallen and his Veng away.

G'vard knelt before his Prime and sought his forgiveness. Galarhade granted it without redress. He told Gabrial to stand. The blue staggered to his feet, the

46

mountain tops dancing around his head. It felt as if his spiracles had been plugged with sand. All three of his hearts were beating fast, and at different rates.

Galarhade called per Grogan forward. To the anxious mentor he said, 'What is your opinion of this?'

Per Grogan gulped. He was one hundred and seventy-four Ki:meran turns old, looking forward to a future of deep simplicity and even deeper sleep. He glanced at the pitiful body of Grystina, mercifully arranged to hide the injuries to her head. He had known this female since she was a myss. How many more lives did this planet have to claim before the Elders looked to colonise elsewhere? A pricking sensation at the corner of one eye warned him of the danger of shedding his fire tear, that drop of burning water that contained a dragon's *auma*, the fire of life granted to them by Godith. 'Gabrial can be…impulsive,' he said. 'A trait inherited from his much-admired father.'

'This is not about his father,' Elder Grynt reminded him.

'I merely wished to point out,' per Grogan said painfully, 'that his father's ability to i:mage was highly developed, if a little…'

'Wild?' said Grynt.

Per Grogan stared at him. He had never liked Grynt.

He was one of those lightly-coloured purple dragons that boasted dark tints and a streak of armoured silver on his throat and breast. He was young for an Elder (a title not awarded purely by age) and had been sent on this mission to oversee security. Although Gallen commanded the Veng in the air, operational procedures were decided by Grynt.

'There is no wickedness in Gabrial,' Grogan said plainly, making sure his voice carried far. 'His loyalty to the Wearle is as true as any dragon. It should not be forgotten that he volunteered for this mission when others suggested he was too young to be of use.'

'And now we see the fruits of it,' Gallen sneered.

Per Grogan turned on the Veng. 'I know this blue. I have trained him well. He would not use his powers of i:maging recklessly.'

For the first time, Elder Givnay entered the debate. Givnay was a mute who had lost the ability to speak due to an accident shortly after birth. He had been trodden on at play by an adult dragon and one side of his throat had collapsed. The injury had left him unable to utter anything other than stifled cries. His fire sacs, still in their early stages of development, had withered to nothing and his chances of making fire were ruined. His devastated father had wanted to end the drake's life, fearing Givnay's future would be a miserable arc of unrequited desires or envies. But the mother's better wishes had prevailed, and despite his difficulties Givnay had grown into a handsome adult – a distinctive grey, with gold and purple trappings around his neck, which helped to shadow the injury he'd sustained. Unlike his peers, he had never roamed or sought the attention of females, but had turned himself inward, developing the skills of the dragon mind. He had spent much time in isolation, meditating upon the glory of Godith and perfecting the gift of *transference*. He could not only speak (and listen) in thoughts, but move his mind into another dragon's head. It was hardly surprising that most dragons feared him. In a world ruled largely by claws and smoke, silence was a weapon not even the Veng knew how to battle.

He leant towards Galarhade and pressed a thought into his mind, which Galarhade aired. 'Did you know what the blue was planning to i:mage?'

Per Grogan looked flustered. His eyes lost focus. Momentarily, his balance faltered. 'I...advised him tactically, of course, but—'

'Advised?' Grynt said, picking out the word and holding it up like a piece of skewered prey.

'Wait,' said Gabrial, stepping up to Grogan's shoulder.

He could see where this line of questioning was going. 'It was my idea to draw G'vard across the crater.'

'You've been warned more than once to be silent,' said Grynt. 'Do I need to remind you, you stand before your Prime? This impertinence will not serve you well.'

'I won't let you hold Grogan to blame,' said Gabrial, the words squirming carelessly out of his mouth.

Every watching dragon caught their breath. To disrespect the Elders in this manner was as good as inviting death's fire to rain down.

'Still – your – voice,' Grynt said, barely needing to open his jaws. Black smoke played around his purple face. 'The per was asked for his opinion and he *alone* shall give it.'

Grogan cleared his throat. Looking squarely at Galarhade, he said, 'I have thought on this and I do not believe my charge was capable of causing a physical eruption. A few live sparks, perhaps, but nothing of the magnitude so witnessed. He's simply not advanced enough.'

Prime Galarhade tilted his head. 'Then what are you saying?'

'That it was a natural event – or that some other force took advantage of the moment.'

Now there were cries of *'Shame!'* from the mountainside.

Elder Grynt leant forward, making his pillar creak beneath his weight. 'Are you accusing a dragon more accomplished of callously causing the death of a queen?' 'Murder' was an ugly word among dragons. Even the Veng did not kill for pleasure or reward.

'Of course not,' Grogan snapped. Raising his voice above the clamour, he roared, 'We were sent to this planet to find the first Wearle! How can we be sure that whatever force has conspired to hide them from us did not bring about the death of Grystina?'

A good argument, but not strong enough to stay the tide of insults.

Only the De:allus dragon, Graymere, was truly taking note of Grogan's words.

In spite of the hysteria, the Elders consulted. The Prime exchanged brief words with Grynt, but spent longer in silent communion with Givnay. In tragic situations such as this, it was Givnay the Wearle would turn to for solace. His long contemplations on the wonders of Godith marked him as a source of spiritual comfort. If any dragon would show mercy, it would be the mute.

Calm fell as Galarhade raised his head. He said,

'We find the blue guilty of causing the rock fall which killed Grystina and her myss. We accept there was no malice intended, and for this reason he is spared the worst of punishments. We also find that the dangers of the i:mage should have been recognised by the per. We therefore hold both to account. Before I pass sentence, would anyone speak in favour of these dragons?'

'I would,' said a voice. To Gabrial's surprise, per Gorst came forward. He was a cousin of Grogan and shared similar gradations in the grey-green blushes that dignified his sides. 'Per Grogan is older than most of my teeth—'

'And nearly as useless,' a Veng voice muttered.

'—but his loyalty to the Wearle is without question. I ask that his sentence be light. As for the blue…yes, he has caused a great misfortune. But let us not forget that he fought to be this queen's companion – and bravely so.'

This was met by another hail of roars.

Per Gorst lengthened his neck and shouted, 'When other, more legitimate candidates, closed their wings and would not even court her!'

Hrrrrrr. The storm of criticism blew itself out.

Per Gorst looked at the dismayed figure of G'vard. 'My charge is wounded, his challenge unfulfilled. But he will recover to fight for another queen. This is a terrible day, I agree. But the Wearle needs young dragons. Fearless dragons. Dragons prepared to face difficult and possibly dangerous encounters. Despite our mapping and our searches we are still no nearer to knowing what happened to the first Wearle. I am therefore in some agreement with Grogan.'

'Your point?' said Grynt.

'I ask that the blue be kept on Erth to continue his work, not exiled back to Ki:mera in shame.'

'I agree,' said Galarhade, before Grynt could interrupt. 'They will both stay – but they must always be reminded of what they have done.' He ordered both dragons to look at him.

Gabrial sat up proudly.

'From this day,' said the Prime, 'until or unless you prove your worth again, you are no longer recognised in the glory of Godith.'

'What does that mean?' said Gabrial.

'It means your name is now Abrial,' said Grynt. He nodded at Grogan. 'And his is Rogan.'

'No,' per Grogan said. His old legs gave way and he collapsed to the stones. This time, not even per Gorst came to help him. 'I am of the old ways. The shame... Please. Anything but this.'

Gabrial glanced at per Gorst. G'vard's second was deeply troubled by the sentence. And very few dragons were making any noise. 'Abrial?' the blue repeated. And then the rumble *did* begin. One of those peculiar waves of sound that dragons could produce, but rarely did.

The sharp and raucous wind of derision.

4

His judgments delivered, Galarhade gave the order that all activities would be postponed until sunrise the next day. During this time the Wearle would pay homage to the memory of Grystina. All of them, Veng included, would return to their settles when the meeting was done to contemplate her life and that of her drake. Elder Givnay would prepare a song of comfort, which he would share with the Wearle through the gift of transference. No dragon would forget this tragic day.

Before that, there was yet more misery for Abrial and Rogan. Looking at the older dragon first, Galarhade decreed that Rogan be removed from his duties as a mapper – one engaged in memorising the layout of the land around the dragons' domayne – and that he be sent instead to the far side of the mountains to mine the seams of fhosforent there. Fhosforent was a pink, crystalline substance found in Erth's volcanic rock. Its discovery had been reported by the first Wearle, who had also determined its principal benefit. Ingesting even minute quantities of the crystals appeared to improve the strength and duration of a dragon's flame. Over the centuries, dragons had tested many naturally-occurring minerals in this manner, but none had produced such rapid or promising effects as fhosforent. Rogan knew the work would be hard, but he was not overly dismayed by his punishment. Confinement in a mine would keep him out of the main body of the Wearle, where there would be fewer taunts about his name. And there was always the chance he might find a rich seam, which would instantly grant him favour with the Elders. In these respects, he counted himself lucky.

Abrial was less enchanted with his new role.

'A sweeper?' he said, when Galarhade passed sentence. Until the morning of the tragedy the young blue had been part of a five-dragon wyng, learning to improve his flying skills. This included lessons in aerial combat from none other than per Gorst. Abrial was easily the best of the wyng and had just advanced to the most exciting part of his training: learning the art of phasing – the ability to move through time during

56

flight. Now, it seemed, his progress was about to be abruptly halted.

'Are you questioning the decision of your Elders?' said Grynt, his breast scales glinting weakly in the sunlight.

'But I was—?'

'It doesn't matter what you *were*. Your duty now is to fly the edges of the domayne, keeping watch for incursions, especially from the Hom. You will rest no more than once on each circuit, and at dawn each day you will report to Veng commander Gallen. Don't disappoint him, blue. The Veng do not respond well to laziness.'

Abrial puffed a heavy wisp of smoke. Talk of the Hom had made his scales lift. He had never seen one of the two-legged creatures that could allegedly stand like bears and make fire *outside* their bodies. (*Hrrr?*) According to per Gorst, who spoke of them occasionally between teaching sessions, their auma levels were superior to any other creature that inhabited Erth (except dragons, of course). The Hom were clever and inventive, he said, but usually fled when challenged. There had only ever been one serious confrontation. Recently, a large Hom male had foolishly hurled a rock at Gallen. The Veng commander had responded with limited force and charred the arm raised against him. But even the Veng adhered to the Elders' law of no killing, except in self-defence or for food. (No dragon had thought to taste the Hom yet, preferring instead to graze on the lush forest greenery or the juicier animal forms that covered the domayne.)

Due to their aggression and relative intelligence, the Hom were chiefly suspected of being involved in the disappearance of the first Wearle, yet nothing could connect them to it. Prime Greffan, in his earliest reports, had identified the Hom as a potential threat. This had first become apparent when he'd ordered his dragons to lay claim to the mountain range. He told how the Hom had resisted being driven out of their caves and how some had fought back with sharpened sticks. No dragons had been injured in the skirmishes and no Hom killed, though several had suffered serious burns when sparks had fallen on their fragile skin or warning flames had blown too close. For a while after the conflict had ended, small parties of Hom had tried to reinvade the domayne. In exasperation, Greffan had ordered his roamers to sear a line in the ground, all the way from the borders of Vargos to the shores of the unmapped sea, a line that the Hom were forbidden to cross. This had led to further clashes, until the Hom had finally withdrawn to resettle in the flat lands beyond the domayne. And there they remained, always a source of simmering tension, without ever posing a serious threat. Barring the incident with Gallen, not a single dragon had since been targeted. The Veng had come to Erth prepared for a fight, but so far their formidable claws had generally been employed picking food off their teeth.

'I thought the Hom were driven out of the domayne?' bickered Abrial, still tetchy about his new role.

'They were,' said Grynt, equally irritable. 'Your job is to stop them coming back *in*.'

'Grynt, be done with this,' said Prime Galarhade. 'We are not gathered here to talk about the Hom.' He gave a call and two more dragons glided down from their settles – the females, Grendel and Gossana. Abrial stepped aside so that Grendel would have room to land. She was a gloriously beautiful dragon with touches of gold around her purple face and enough lytes underwing to star the night sky. Her eyes, like Abrial's, were just beginning to crystallise, but there was still enough softness in them to melt even the hardest of Veng hearts. She nodded shyly at Abrial, a look that suggested she felt sorry for him. He gulped and tightened his wings. Being this close to Grendel made his scales rattle, and that was not wise in front of the Elders.

The other female, Gossana, was well known throughout the Wearle. She was dark green, running to black along her neck. She had heavily-slanted eyes, one the colour of amber stones, the other near blood red. Many dragons feared to look at her, for the eyes could alter colour with her mood. Like most mature females, she possessed a ruffle of sawfin scales, which stood up in a frill behind her ears and were the same dark colour as the rest of her body. This bestowed her with a bold, majestic look, which she further inflated with the high carriage of her head. On Ki:mera she had twice raised wearlings and had been sent to Erth to oversee Grystina's first birthing – a slightly modest assignation for one so grand, but an important commission nonetheless. Galarhade bowed when he spoke to her.

'Matrial,' he said, acknowledging her previous successes with young.

'A sorry day,' she said, funnelling dark smoke. Dark smoke was heavier than air and would fall from the nostrils rather than drift away. It was one of the few ways a dragon could express sorrow. She glanced at Grynt and the ever-silent Givnay. Both gave a courteous nod.

'We have a problem,' said Galarhade. 'Grystina's wearmyss is without a mother. I cannot commit her body to Godith until we have settled upon a solution.'

'Is it so difficult?' Gossana said, her words almost hissing across the water. If any other dragon had addressed the Prime so, they would have been met with an ear-singeing flame. (Abrial actually flinched, expecting it.) 'We have an able female in Grendel. Fostering an orphan is not beyond her, as long as the myss is given to her quickly. I'm surprised the Elders have been slow to see this.'

'I see it,' said Galarhade, some authority restored in his terse response. He straightened his long red neck. 'The myss is sickly, her air sacs full of dust. She is nesting in healer Grymric's cave. She will be given over to one of you when Grymric is satisfied she will survive.'

'One of us?' Gossana said. She inhaled the last of her smoke.

'It is important,' Galarhade said, letting some weight fall onto his words, 'that we continue our breeding programme.'

'One of us?' Gossana repeated, her upper jaw pulled so tight that her teeth were now aggressively unveiled. A broken fang on the upper left side was causing an abrasion where it met the lower jaw, weeping saliva and a touch of green blood. 'Are you saying you expect *me* to foster the myss?' Her fin scales billowed.

Abrial shuddered and looked around him. G'vard and per Gorst were keeping their silence. Even Grynt was curling his claws.

Elder Givnay leant towards his Prime, who nodded as he received a thought from the mute. Galarhade said, 'The Elders acknowledge Gossana's past accomplishments and are grateful she brings her wisdom and experience to bear at this time. However, as Elder Givnay has reminded me, we must always introduce new lines into the Wearle. We are therefore decided that Grendel will enter the next laying cycle and Gossana will raise the myss.'

'This is an insult!' Gossana roared.

'It is my ruling,' Galarhade said firmly.

'Yours – or his?' She cocked her snout in the direction of Givnay. She had never liked the mute, whom she saw as little more than an ineffective peddler of spiritual fantasies. What use, she had been known to argue, was a dragon steered by its third (and smallest) heart? The matrial had even been recorded as saying that she would not have let Givnay survive the injury that had left him unable to flame or speak. Not surprisingly, there was little regard between them. What *was* surprising was that both had been included in the second Erth party, a decision that had caused a great deal of muttering among some orders of the Wearle.

Despite Gossana's fearless conceit, Elder Grynt felt it necessary to lash out a warning. 'Have a care, Matrial. Remember where you are.'

Gossana spread her gigantic wings, almost blowing Abrial off his feet. 'Have you forgotten that I am *frenhines fawr*?' (Words from the old tongue, meaning 'great queen'.) 'How dare you dishonour me like this? The fostering of orphans is for common dragons, not one of *my* standing. And what male would willingly protect an orphan's…carer?!'

Galarhade let out a thread of steam. 'The white, G'vard, will be your guardian, and will be called father to the myss.'

This raised an immediate objection from per Gorst. 'Prime, with respect, that cannot be. The battle was void.'

'Well, it appears he's been declared the winner,' snapped Grynt, who seemed to be growing tired of the arguments.

'But without her true mother to imprint upon, the character of the wearmyss will always be challenged. This would be of little importance if the father was of less noble bearing, but—'

'It's all right, Gorst, I will do it,' said G'vard. He raised his weary head. 'In the name of Godith, I will honour Grystina and be a father to her myss.' He looked at Gossana and bowed. 'I pledge to protect you in all—'

'Faah!' said Gossana. 'Save your voice for singing your orphan to sleep. I demand to be returned to Ki:mera,' she roared. 'You'll send the wearling too, if you know what's good for it.'

'You would be wise to bite your tongue,' said Grynt – a slightly inappropriate remark, given the condition of Gossana's upper fangs.

She bared the whole row at him. 'You haven't heard the last of this.' And with a screech that made the mountains shudder, she took off back to her eyrie.

Abrial sank into a pit of despair. His wings felt as heavy as the rain clouds looming overhead. Had it not been for a kind glance from Grendel, he might have thrown himself under the waterfall and joined the ice on its long trail down to the sea.

Prime Galarhade called for Grendel's attention. The young female looked up, her blue eyes lively with fear. Galarhade said, 'Be calm, Grendel. Do not think yourself unworthy of the duty your Elders have placed upon you. Although you were not brought here to further the early growth of the Wearle, fate has selected you to be the first true queen of this colony. You were born of noble, Fissian ancestors. The males that come to you must be a suitable match. Do you understand?'

'Yes.' The word clicked in her throat.

'Are you ready to be courted?'

'I am.' She bowed before Galarhade, but again she flashed a look at Abrial as if to say, *Will you fly with me?*

It made his hearts race to have her regard, but it also hurt so much. How he would have loved to chase Grendel round the mountains. But what chance would he have, stuck out on the edge of the domayne, keeping watch? He was going to be a sweeper, the lowest of the low. A forest might have grown on the peak of Skytouch before he ever saw Grendel again.

With a *whumph!* Grystina's body caught fire. Galarhade was above her, coating her in flame. One by one every dragon flew past, adding their own breath to the blaze.

'Forgive me,' Abrial whispered. And he lifted up and flamed Grystina as well, not caring who was watching or what was being said. And when his flame was spent he lifted up again and flew away from the lake. He glided over the bulging crags of Vargos, setting a course for the northernmost edge of the domayne. He hung his head low as he flew. His life was over, he told himself. His name was blunted, his family shamed, his chances of fathering wearlings minimal. It really didn't get much worse than this.

But had he been a little less doleful and a little more alert, his life would have been so very, very different. Had he chanced to begin his sweep from that moment, his sensitive optical triggers would surely not have missed a slight movement on the hillside, the actions of a creature desperate to conceal itself against the dark rock. Unbeknown to the dragons, the loss of Grystina was being felt by something other than themselves.

A young Hom was on the mountainside. A boy, no more than twelve winters old. Within the folds of his robe he was hiding something.

A frightened dragon wearling.

A drake.

Part Two

Ren

5

It was forbidden, by order of Targen the Old. No man or woman of the tribe must contest the beasts or defy their will. Just to look upon the skalers, especially in flight, was enough to call down their fire on the tribe. From now on, men would settle on the flatlands.

This was the law of the Kaal.

Ren Whitehair, son of Ned, heard the words true. No man or woman must contest the beasts. But Targen the Old had not mentioned boys. And what kind of boy concerned himself with laws when his heart was beating to the spirit of adventure?

Ever since the first group had burst through the sky and driven the Kaal tribe out of the mountains, the beasts had been despised by the men. A few brave souls had crossed the scorch line in defiance, but all had returned to the settlement in terror, many with hot blood running from their ears, clouds across their vision or blisters on their skin. Thus far, the skalers had killed no men, but their forceful defence of the mountain territories suggested they would burn to the bones anyone foolish enough to provoke them to excess. Nothing got past their patrols anyway. The eyes of the beasts were so advanced it was said they could see the smallest scratcher scurrying through grass from the highest clouds above. And even if a man did manage to hide, he could not conceal the scent of his body.

But as much as men mourned the loss of their caves, it was all Ren could do to contain his excitement about the skalers. Awed by their power, he was eager to be near them and learn their ways. He was often chastised by his father for climbing to high places from which he might watch them, and banned from making drawings of the beasts. 'What Kaal,' Ned had thundered in exasperation, 'would wish to look upon a rock and see the eyes of a skaler looking back?'

None of this hampered Ren's ambitions. If a curfew was placed upon him, he simply waited out his father's temper and amused himself with the cache of skaler artefacts he kept hidden among the hides on which he slept: two talons, a chipped scale that sparkled under

70

moonlight, and the charred bones of several unfortunate animals. What would it feel like, he wondered, to run his hand along a whole row of scales? Or ride upon a beast as it soared above the mountains? Such fancies played with his dreams, but dreams were all they were destined to be, until the morning of the fateful hunt, the day he saw Utal Longarm burn.

Ren had been out catching snorters with the men when two huge skalers had ranged across the sky. Utal had dared to challenge them. Utal, who stood higher than any man in the tribe, had ripped his robe wide open at the neck, bared his chest and roared at the beasts to give the mountains back to the Kaal.

Ned, who was leading the hunt that morning, turned his whinney round and said, 'Utal, step back from the line. If you bring the beasts down, we all burn.'

But Utal had been drinking the juice of many berries and his head was not where it needed to be. He began to dance and sing a lewd song. Stomping left and right, he flapped his arms in a mocking imitation of beating wings. 'Harken to me, skaler! I'm flying!' he boomed.

It amused the men, but not Ren's father, who was watching the beasts with a wary eye. 'Oak,' he said, to the man astride the whinney nearest him, 'I propose you tie your brother to his mount if you wish to hear him snoring tonight.'

Oak laughed and pulled on his reins. 'Utal, stand back,' he called. 'Ned fears you might be worrying the beasts. Don't poison them with your breath, brother!'

It was a decent attempt to calm the situation, but Utal continued his clownish antics. And now Ren was growing concerned for him as well. A skaler the colour of fresh spring grass was raising the horns that grew in sharp lines from the back of its head. Ren had seen many skalers do this just before they swept to take prey.

The beast was preparing to attack.

'Utal, it's coming!' he called.

Still Utal refused to listen. He lifted a foot and dangled it over the scorch line. Then he pulled up the lower half of his robe and made water on the skalers' territory.

The bright green beast gave a quiet snarl and bared more fangs than Ren could count. Almost leisurely, it glided down and produced a burst of fire that made the hair crackle on Utal's head. Utal yelped. And then he *really* danced, flapping his arms as if a swarm of buzzers had filled his ears. Foolishly, he picked up a stone.

His brother whispered, 'Utal, no…'

But the fool could not resist. He took aim and hurled

the stone. It bounced harmlessly off the skaler's rump. The beast flicked its tail in anger. Utal gave a triumphant shout and picked up another, larger stone.

This one would never leave his hand.

The green beast circled back. It put itself directly in line with Utal and began what appeared to be another slow descent. It was still some distance away and there was time enough for Utal to halt his madness. But Ren had witnessed this manoeuvre as well. He had once seen a beast bear down on a bleater, closing so fast that the hapless animal had died of fright, even before the claws sank into it. He knew exactly what was going to happen.

'GET DOWN!' he screamed.

At the same time Oak kicked his whinney in the belly and raced toward his brother. He planned to knock some sense into the oaf or at best take hold of his newly-singed hair and drag him clear of the line. But in an instant the beast was there in front of them, fearfully huge, much closer to the line than anyone (other than Ren) had expected. It had somehow jumped the length of fifty men in the time it would have taken Ren to crush a leaf in the palm of his hand. The whinneys reared. The men yelped in terror. Ren flung himself down as the beast unlatched its blistering jaws and released another surge of flame. The fire travelled in a ball from the back of its throat and burst against Utal's upright arm, charring it black from the midbone to the hand. Utal rocked like a blade of grass. His eyes glazed, their centres stopped. Then he fell in a slow and steady motion. He sagged to his knees and toppled sideways, falling just the right side of the scorch line.

The skaler banked away, splattering sizzling dung across the field. One pat landed squarely on Utal, steaming where it glued to the skin of his chest. The men recovered their nerve and dragged him away. Using leaves, they cleaned off what they could of the dung, cursing when it stung their hands. Then they laid Utal over a whinney and quickly took him back to the settlement. One burst of lunacy had bought their best hunter a withered arm and a new name. From then on he was known as Utal Stonehand, because the stone he'd intended to throw was now permanently fused to his clawed black fist.

And there was worse. By the time the men had laid him out, the stains of the dung had burned into his chest, eating back the flesh in great red welts. A splash had travelled to his eye as well, fusing the lid to the ball in a horrible stew. And no amount of bathing could wash the stench of dung off his body. Poor Utal. He now had a chest that stank, a useless arm and only one eye to see it with. The stench made certain no one visited his shelter without good cause, and not without their face wrapped heavily in cloth. It was a terrible lesson to bear, and Targen the Old was rightfully enraged. Had he not ordered the Kaal to stay clear of the beasts? Was it not better to live in peace beyond the mountains rather than be walking ash among them? The men glumly acknowledged this wisdom, but the incident had rankled their pride and there was much shared talk that night about what might be done to restore their honour. The beasts were mocking them. First they had driven the tribe from the mountains, and now left their best man ruined by dung!

But while most of the Kaal tribe cussed and wailed, Ren began to look at what else might be learned from this dreadful incident – and a frightening idea came to him. It happened as he watched Oak Longarm burning his brother's soiled robe. Even in the fire the bad odour still carried, blocking out the cooking smells around the camp. Men and women alike were complaining, covering their noses as they went about their work. It made Ren wonder how the skalers put up with it, never mind the Kaal – and suddenly, there it was: a way of reaching the mountains again, a way of getting close to the beasts.

Use *dung*.

It would be dangerous. Ridiculously so. One mistake and Ren would be black specks floating on the wind. But the challenge burned so brightly in his mind that he could not resist exploring it. Early the next morning, he crept back toward the mountains and waited until the skies were clear. Then he ran across the scorch line in search of what he needed – a fresh heap of skaler dung.

The heap he found was fresher than fresh, steaming black, still red with cinders. It almost boiled away the mitt he'd made for his hands. Turning his face aside, he smeared the dung over a robe he'd brought with him. Oh, it smelled bad. Worse than the innards of a dying mutt. But he stuck to the task and when it was done he undressed and put the dung robe on, over an undercloth he'd stolen from his mother's things. She would roast him like a snorter if she ever found out, but Ren had taken note of Utal's suffering and knew he must keep the dung off his skin. Thankfully, the extra layer worked, but the stench was just as bad as ever. Every time Ren drew breath, the reek almost tore the nose off his face. But the deed was done and there was no going back. Two beasts had appeared above the shoulder of the mountains. He was over the scorch line, inside their territory. Now he must hide – or die.

Throwing the clean robe aside, he sank into a small depression in the rocks, drawing up the bare parts of his legs and covering his face with a shallow-rooted thicket he'd ripped from the ground. The beasts soon saw the robe he'd discarded. One of them, a bright green monster identical to the one that had maimed Utal, dropped with a heavy thump beside the cloth while the other glided in circles overhead. The beast picked up the robe and sniffed it. It turned its incredible head both ways, staring left and right along the hillside. The eye that Ren could just about see rolled suspiciously in its socket, the inner layers moving like ripples on a pond. Ren steadied his breathing, praying he hadn't left a toe exposed. He thought about his hair, which was lighter than the colour of corn, and hoped the thicket had covered it well. *Lay still*, he told himself. *Still as the dead.* If he rattled the thicket or made water down his leg he would know in an instant what it felt like to be a log on a fire.

But the beast didn't come for him, and its friend in the sky was growing impatient. It gave a grating call. The one on the hill gave a sharp call back. It took off with a *whumph!*, trying to shake the robe from its claws. It was several wingbeats clear of the hill before the robe came sailing back. It landed beside Ren's hiding place, ripped but still wearable.

When he was certain the skalers had gone, Ren carefully changed back and hid the soiled robe beneath the thicket, keeping it separate from the undercloth. A flush of boyish pride ran through him. He had accomplished something no one else in the tribe had ever done. He had walked across the scorch line and back again, unburned.

He had fooled the beasts.

6

Ren hurried back to the settlement and washed for some time in the river which ran behind the shelters, treading water in the shadow of an overhanging tree to avoid inquisitive eyes. Very little of the dung had got onto his hands (one slight burn on a fingertip) and mercifully the smell stayed in the water. He walked home fresh of body and mind, bristling with the need to tell someone what he'd done. Wisely, however, he kept it to himself, mainly because he returned to find the settlement veiled in sadness.

Utal had developed a fever. No one would speak any details of it, but Ren heard his father saying to his mother that Utal's arm was being chewed by a wound the colour of grass. None of Targen's herbs could cleanse it. Two days later, Utal died. His wounded eye was sealed and matted, the other popping out like a hard grey pebble.

The tribe gathered around a fire to mourn him. They drank the juice of many berries. The talk among the men grew loud and dangerous. They shook spears at the mountains and called for vengeance. But what hope did they have of killing a skaler when they could not even get near to the beasts?

This was the moment an unexpected voice spoke up.

'Ren Whitehair knows a way.'

The voice belonged to a girl, Pine Onetooth, so called because she had one strong tooth in the middle of her mouth, gaps to either side of it.

'What's this?' said Ned, while Ren was busy stilling his heart.

Pine came into the light. A frail girl, thin as the flower stalk hanging loose between her fingers. 'Two days afore, I see'd him washin' long in the river.'

'Washing?' scoffed Ned. 'Away with you, girl. The boy's mother likens him most to a snorter. If he could bathe his bones in mud, he would do it.'

The men laughed, but Oak Longarm took up Pine's words. 'What mean you, Pine? Why would seeing Ren in the river be aught to do with the skalers?'

Pine did not answer. She simply looked at Ren and skipped away into the night.

'Well?' said Oak. He turned his attention now upon the boy.

But Ned Whitehair was in no mood to amuse himself with the ways of children. 'Ren, be gone. Your bed beckons,' he said. He flicked a twig into the fire and ran a hand through his hair. The loss of Utal had hit him hard.

'Nay, I would hear his piece,' said Oak. 'The boy is quick of mind and purpose.'

This was met with a grunt from Oak's right. Varl Rednose, a man with an oval belly and a beard so dense it was a wonder nothing nested there said, 'Perhaps your boy would tell us our business, Ned? Shall I loan him a spear and point him at the mountains? He might bring us back a juicy skaler leg to roast.' He broke wind, making the fire flutter. The men laughed loudly, but their mood remained sour.

Ned said, 'Varl, he's a boy. Let him be.'

'Aye, but he likes the beasts fondly, doesn't he?' Varl stared at Ren as if he meant the lad mischief. 'Why do you stand among the grieving, boy, when your heart flies the other side of the scorch line?'

'Ned!' Oak gripped Ned's arm before he could retaliate. 'What good would it do to fight among ourselves? How will that bring my brother justice?'

Varl burped and wiped an arm across his mouth. 'I tell you all there will be no justice until we put a sword through a skaler's throat. But let us hear what Whitehair's boy has to say. My gut is sore in need of humour.'

'Well?' said Ned. He switched his gaze to his son.

The eyes of the Kaal tribe turned upon Ren, pressing the story out of him.

'I…I know a way to cross the line safe,' he said.

'What?' said Ned. 'What blether is this?'

'Ned, give him air,' Oak Longarm said. He met Ren's gaze again. 'You have made your boast, Ren, now you must share it.'

Ren could feel himself shaking inside. There was a terrible, terrible conflict here. If he did not say his piece he would be sorely ridiculed before his father. But if he revealed his method to the men, he was opening up the way for a possible attack on the creatures he loved. But what if the Kaal did cross into skaler territory? One man? Two men? A whole tribe? What harm could they do to the winged giants?

And so he spoke his truth. 'Dung,' he said.

A portion of the fire collapsed, scattering cinders across the erth.

'Dung?' Varl said. 'Have my ears turned soft?' He stood up, swaying. 'DUNG?' he thundered. 'Are you mocking us, boy? It was dung that took out Utal's eye!' He hurled a stale, chewed bone at Ren, and not even Ned could object to it.

'But...it works,' Ren shouted over their derision. He looked at Oak, who had turned his head away in disappointment. 'I covered a robe in their scent and went beyond the line. I hid from two of the beasts – and returned.'

Ned stood up quickly, forcing Ren back. 'Go to your bed and dream there,' he snarled. 'What devil makes you shame me so? This, on a day so clouded by misery?'

'But—?'

'Go!' Ned pointed the way.

Ren sighed and stumbled back. But he did not go to his bed, for a storm was brewing in the minds of the men and the first roll of thunder was about to break. It came from the mouth of Varl Rednose again. 'Why do we sit with our hearts in our boots when we all know a way to defeat the skalers?' He cast his ugly gaze around the circle. 'I will not sleep this night while these words sit heavy on my tongue: I say we raise the darkeyes.'

'NO!' cried Ren, coming forward again.

Once more, his father was forced to intervene. He grabbed a hunk of Ren's robe and drew the boy to him. 'This is men's talk. Why are you still here?'

Ren shook his head, making his white hair fly. 'Please, Pa. You cannot let them do this.'

But the plot was already in progress. 'How?' said Oak, the only voice except Varl's not muttering in fear.

Varl clapped a hand to Oak's sturdy shoulder. 'Utal's spirit may be with the Fathers, but his body can still be of use to us.'

Oak looked puzzled. 'Again, I ask how?'

Varl bent close. 'We give your brother to the darkeyes in sacrifice.'

'What?' said Oak. His face had turned the colour of the moon.

Varl straightened up. 'We go to their cave,' he boomed at the men. 'We wake them, aye. Make them know the skalers are back. Invite them to suck every speck of green from that murderous fire-thrower in the mountains. Let the darkeyes and skalers war again. Let the beasts be hunted by the black terror and the skies be clear of their kind for good – just like the first time the skalers came…'

'No!' cried Ren. 'I won't let you hurt them! It was Utal's folly that earned him the right to his walk with death. The skalers mean us no harm!'

'Ned, put your boy away,' growled Varl.

And Ned had no choice but to drag Ren clear.

At the shelter, he drew the boy to him again. 'Listen to me, Ren, and listen well. Is your mind so addled by these fearful creatures that you have no pity for Oak's sad loss and would taunt a brute like Rednose with it? I have no love for the darkeyes, you know this. I would rather swallow a fistful of grit than have the tribe befriend such a hideous thing. But the skalers have taken Utal's life. We must fight for his honour. What else would you have me do?'

'Make peace,' gulped Ren.

Ned sighed and put a hand to the boy's pale face, wiping away a tear with his thumb. 'The skalers took our land, Ren. The stars were always going to settle like this.'

'Then you will all *die!*' Ren said harshly.

And he dived into the shelter and threw himself, face down, onto his bed.

That night, without sleep, Ren thought long about the 'black terror', for the darkeyes were a mystery all to themselves.

Sometime after the first wave of skalers, the Kaal began to witness battles taking place in the skies above the mountains. A terrifying creature, the colour of a caarker but the size of twenty, appeared just as suddenly as the beasts had done. They had twisted, scale-free bodies, stunted wings and a shortened tail. Their eyes were like mud shaken up in water; no light shone from their fixed black cores. They blew no fire, these things, but instead released a poisonous spit that burned as fiercely as any flame. Several of the tribe carried scars from the time a squealing darkeye had crashed on the settlement, the rear half of its body ablaze. Ren's father had put an arrow through its throat as it thrashed in agony on the ground. He'd been trying to show the creature mercy, but the darkeye had let out a hideous squeal, thrown its head and sprayed the camp with its ugly bile. A skaler had followed the darkeye down and destroyed it with a flame so hot it had marked a deep scar in the ground. Whatever these dark-eyed creatures were, the skalers regarded them as mortal enemies.

The battles raged for nearly three days. No man or woman of the Kaal (and certainly not Ren) ever believed the skalers would be beaten. Yet they were. The darkeyes prevailed, with two survivors. It was feared the two would lay claim to the land and call others of their kind to colonise the mountains. But no. More mystery followed. The survivors withdrew, secreting themselves in a cave half a day's ride from the settlement. They were still there now as far as anyone knew, yet they had not challenged the new crop of skalers. Likewise, the second wave of skalers seemed unaware of the enemy in the cave. A bizarre situation, but one that the Kaal, led by Varl Rednose, intended to use to their advantage.

The next morning, Ren heard more of their scheme. Varl announced it openly to the tribe. Let the darkeyes have Utal! Let his body be taken to their cave and shown to the creatures! They will know from the stink, if not the arm, that skalers are in the air again! Surely this will draw them out and encourage them to drive their enemy away!

The Kaal roared their support, but nothing could be done without Targen's approval.

Targen retired to consider the plan. He would speak in dreams with the Fathers, he said, and announce his decision shortly. The men chewed on their frustration. They were ready to tie poor Utal to a sled and drag him to the darkeyes there and then. But Targen had spoken, and they must wait.

Ren was relieved. Here was his chance to act. If Targen's journey with the Fathers was long (and they usually were), Ren would have time to carry out a plan of his own, one he'd been hatching overnight.

Under the hides where his father slept was a rare prize. When the burning darkeye had crashed on the settlement, some kind of horn had broken from its head and lodged in the wall of Ned Whitehair's shelter. A small, hardened spiral of flesh, sharper at its tip than the best Kaal arrows. Ren had wanted it for his collection, but to his frustration, his father had claimed it. A trophy, Ned said, for arrowing the beast. It was the best relic in the Kaal's possession, the only evidence they had of the darkeyes' existence.

Before he departed, Ren left a flower on his mother's bed, hoping she would send his soul to the Fathers if he was brought back to her in a worse state than Utal. In truth, he could not explain this feeling in his breast, but his heart told him he must do right. His plan was simple. When night fell he would cross the scorch line, make his way to the great ice lake, bow down before the skalers and show them the horn.

The darkeyes were coming. The beasts needed to be warned.

And he, Ren Whitehair, would be the one to do it.

7

He used the dung robe as he had before. The smell had turned even worse for the keeping, but this was the price Ren knew he must pay if he wanted to get among the beasts.

The night was dry and idly dark. Even the sluggish, half-chewed moon failed to notice him crossing the scorch line. Only twice did he need to conceal himself, once from a startled hooter that glided away from the smell of his disguise, and once from a distant skaler. This time, the beast made no attempt to land.

By dawn, he was deep into skaler territory, already climbing the sleeping mountain, so called because it rumbled with fire and smoke like an old man blowing wind from either end of his body. The beasts were often seen circling here. Skalers, because of their size and weight, needed good ledges on which to settle. And nowhere were the mountainsides more ragged than on the peaks that surrounded the great ice lake. Ren was certain he would find a whole clutch of skalers here. And why warn one when he might warn many?

Travelling in the light was slow and dangerous. For a while, he was safe in the Whispering Forest, among the swathe of tall green spikers that thrived on the lowest sections of the climb. But when the trees thinned out and he was faced with a bumpy expanse of grass, his choices became severely limited. If a skaler flew over and he was forced to lie low, he would have to hope it mistook him for a solitary stone. A perilous risk to take. So he changed his mind and took the longer way round, keeping to those areas of bare grey rock where only the skinniest plants took hold and the shadows offered plenty of cover.

Despite the unevenness of the slope, he was able to travel freely for a while. But it wasn't long before the mountain grew serious and the rise began to bow his back. The rocks made ever more awkward angles and their edges began to cut into his hands. And soon he was faced with another problem: snow. The higher he climbed, the more pockets he encountered. At first he ignored it and went scrambling up the incline like a young bleater; the Kaal were mountain people, used to living with cold conditions. But there came a point where every fingerhold burned. Worse, water had leaked into his boots. His toes no longer moved when he stretched them and his back was a growing arc of pain. If he didn't complete his journey soon he would either have to go back to the settlement or make himself known to the next beast that flew over.

Luck was on his side, however. Not far ahead was a fresh crop of trees. They were set out in clusters of twos and threes. Their branches were sparse and offered poor cover, but no skaler, unless it came down to feed, was going to see him amongst them.

He checked the skies then ran for the nearest tree. It wasn't easy. The slope was truly against him now and his knees had forgotten how to bend. Twice he stumbled, the second time kicking enough scree down the mountain to wake every beast from the ice lake to the sea. The rubble slid away and would not stop clattering. Ren plunged toward the treeline, getting there in time to see a purple skaler with a long white neck come soaring up the spur of the hill. It jerked its head at the trickle of stones, but didn't stop to investigate. Ren sighed with relief and pressed back against a tree. A chance to rest and warm his hands.

Burying his fingers in the pits of his arms, he turned to see where the skaler had gone. It was well above the ridge, near the peak of the mountain, resting on an overhang beside another skaler. They snapped at each other as they shuffled for room. Then both of them turned toward the valley, their long tails flapping in the wind.

At the same time, a lengthy cry split the air. Ren jumped and covered his ears. The wail was so strong it shook the trees, sending down a shower of the dark green spikes that grew from their branches. A skaler had clearly made the sound, but it seemed to have come from *within* the mountain. The pair high above roared back in response. Ren's heart began to thump in unison. He didn't need to speak the skalers' language to realise they were seized with excitement.

Blowing on his hands he moved into the open, scrabbling from one clump of trees to the next. A half-blind caarker might see him now, but the skalers seemed more concerned with what was happening on the far side of the ridge than in guarding this tiny part of their territory. At the last of the trees, Ren paused for breath, and looking up, he saw an amazing sight.

Two skalers, one white, one blue, appeared to be clashing in mid-air. They rolled as they approached one another at speed, disappearing from sight as a cloud exploded and the sky around them filled with rain.

Ren had never seen a spectacle like it.

He hurried on again, hugging the final bend in the hill that would take him swiftly to the top of the ridge. But at its steepest the hill puckered gently inward, and he was irritated to find that he needed to climb a short, almost vertical wall of rock. Desperate not to miss too much of the fight, he reached up and found the holds he needed. At no point did it occur to him that this might be a reckless venture. Indeed, it wasn't until he was halfway to the top that his folly was realised and the first note of panic set in. *Whup! Whup! Whup!* A skaler was approaching. Ren's heart immediately beat a new rhythm. Breathless with fright, he looked over his shoulder. The thing was out of sight, somewhere behind a bulge in the hill. But the onrushing clatter of wings suggested it would fill the sky at any moment. Ren was in a hopeless position, his arms and legs both fully exposed. If he was seen – and the skaler would have to be blind to miss him – the beast could melt him with an arc of flame. Frantically, he looked for somewhere to hide. Again, his luck was in. Down to his right the rock face darkened and he could see a crescent-shaped split in the stone. Using all his strength he swung himself sideways and dropped onto a sill just in front of the split, gouging his left knee as he fell. It was all he could do not to cry out in pain. Somehow, he managed to grip his knee before the blood could bubble freely to the surface and send its warm scent into the air. He rolled into the opening, out of sight. The skaler flew past, blowing up a cloud of dust and grit. Ren stalled for as long as he could before opening his lungs and coughing out the dirt. The skaler was gone by then, but something had heard Ren's burst of noise. A growl, not unlike a row of deep clicks, came creeping out of the belly of the mountain. Ren turned his head and stared into the darkness. There was something in here.

Something huge.

8

That was the moment Ren should have escaped, while the skalers were diverted by the fight above the valley. He should have dressed his wound, counted his blessings and fled. Blood was leaking fast through his fingers. His lungs were lined with grime and dust. Climbing was going to be painful at best. And he didn't need Targen the Old to tell him that whatever had made that clicking sound would not stop to think about taking off his head if he poked it close within biting range.

He stared into the darkness again. By now his eyes were making use of the light and he could see he was in a narrow cleft, no wider than his outstretched arms could span. The crack ran some way into the mountain, tightening at its end where the light grew dim. With the skalers occupied, Ren slid down and attended to his wound. The gash was the length of his smallest finger and dark with grit at its puffiest end. He picked out as many chips as he could, then spat on his hand and rubbed the spittle into the cut. It stung like the tips of a hundred spikers, so sharp he couldn't stop himself yelping. Again the darkness answered, with a growl even more threatening than the last. But on top of the warning was a grating squeal that could only have come from the throat of something small. Ren's heart pounded again. For now he had guessed what was in the mountain: a female skaler, maybe with young.

It was madness, he knew, to even think of going closer. He had once seen his mother give birth to a child (a brother that had not survived) and she had screamed foul murder at any man who tried to approach, especially Ren's father. But Ren had also known the joy of seeing and holding a new-born mutt, and the lure of the skalers proved too much. Quickly, he tore off a piece of his under-robe (the cleanest patch he could find) and tied it tightly around his knee. Then he hopped to his feet and started to feel his way along the cleft. The light from outside was quick to grow faint, but he was soon drawn forward by a deeper, yellower glow. It occurred to him that it must be fire, because the air all around was thick and warm and seemed to be competing for his every breath. On he went, aware that the passage was leading him down, until sixty paces forward, his progress was stopped. A wedge of stone was blocking the upper half of the cave, creating what amounted to a tunnel beneath it. The only way through was on his belly or his back.

He got down and squeezed himself into the hole. The first push was the hardest, but once his shoulders were beyond the wedge the tunnel became a comfortable crawl. It took two painful scrapes off his arms, but the threat of small flesh wounds was soon to be the least of his worries. At its end, the tunnel opened out again. And there, almost filling the entire floor space of a huge cavern, was a beautiful skaler.

She was mid-green with white flecks around her head. Her incredible slanted eyes were the colour of the setting sun, but shone in all directions like broken ice. Ren could see her as clearly as day, thanks to a cluster of small fires burning low along the scorch-blackened stone behind her. It took him a moment to realise she was burning her own waste matter. It occurred to him then that she must have scented the dung on his robe. But if she knew he was there, she seemed unconcerned. She was curled up like a sleeping mutt, tenderly nosing a large blue egg that had just cracked open at its narrowest point. A tiny skaler, purple in colour, was struggling to break out. The mother whispered her encouragement and bathed the egg in a pale half-flame. The shell crackled and split in several places. A tail poked out, followed by a wing. The youngster shuddered and the shell exploded off its body. Ren held his breath in wonder. This was better than he ever could have hoped. To see a mother and—

Suddenly a second youngster clambered onto a rock in front of him. It was blue, this one, with wings the colour of black thornberries. Although Ren was still in shadow, the young skaler clearly had his scent. It flipped its head to one side and sniffed. Out of its throat came a weak roar. *Grrrockle.*

Ren took a breath. It was almost his last. Faster than an arrow, the mother's tail lifted and shot towards the tunnel. Ren saw it coming and scrabbled back in time to avoid being speared. He realised then that she'd been waiting for him, working out precisely where he was before she struck.

The skaler's tail lashed around the walls, its sharp points drilling into the darkness, stirring up another stifling dust cloud. Ren coughed and pressed back as far as he could, the tail twisting like a fire sprite in front of him. But for a bend in the tunnel, he would have been skewered like a roasting snorter. Maybe the skaler thought so too, for as she pulled her tail clear Ren heard her move and guessed she was turning, ready to fill the tunnel with flame. From that, there would be no escape. The flame would travel like a gush of water and make ash of anything it found in the space.

Ren slid down and covered his eyes. He begged the Fathers to forgive his folly and prayed that his mother would not weep long. A moment passed. But the fire did not come. The skaler moved again. And now she was not the only thing shifting. Ren could feel his entire body shaking, but fear was only part of the cause. He touched the wall behind him. The rock was trembling. Grit fell from a crack in the stone above his head.

The sleeping mountain was waking up.

The skaler knew it too. She let out another screaming call, so loud Ren thought his chest would burst. Silence thickened around him for a moment, as if he'd put his head in a bucket of mud. Again, the wall behind him shook. Dizzy with fear, he struggled to his feet.

He needed to escape, that much was clear. But as he turned he heard a pitiful cry. He knew right away that one of the new-born skalers was in trouble. The voice of survival urged him to go, but that bleat had torn a hole in his heart. In truth, he owed the beasts nothing. They would kill him as soon as look at him. But the code of honour that governed all life had been drilled into Ren from a very young age. *All life is precious*, his father had taught him. For Ren, that included the lives of skalers. He couldn't desert the youngster now.

He staggered back to the lip of the tunnel. Rocks were falling like hard black rain, pounding the mother as she sought in vain to protect her young. She was curling her tail around the skaler that Ren had seen breaking from the egg and was all the while calling the blue one to her. Ren could see it, trapped in rubble, kicking its tiny skaler feet. One wing and half its body was buried. The mountain yawned. More rocks fell. A huge lump struck the mother on the head. She lurched forward and her skin split open. Dark green fluid poured out of the wound, coating her neck and the stones around her. Ren thought he saw a tear begin to form in her eye. A single tear, glowing with fire.

That was it. He leapt into the cavern. It took a heartbeat, no more, to free the skaler. It squealed like an angry storm of caarkers, but folded its wings as he drew it to his breast.

Through the hail and dust, he looked for the other. It was sheltered by a curl of the mother's tail. Thinking he could place the rescued one with it, Ren started to pick his way back toward them. But the sleeping mountain was wide awake now. The floor of the cavern whined and split open. Ren was thrown back as a crack the size of a narrow stream divided him from the mother skaler. Pained and spluttering, he got to his feet. The youngster had fixed its claws into his robe as if begging him never to leave it, but the mother was slipping away. One last time she lifted her head – and fixed her gaze on Ren.

Her thoughts poured into his mind with such force that his neck almost snapped as his head jerked back. And these three words she spoke without speaking: *GALAN AUG SCIETH.*

Then her head slackened and thumped against the stone.

With a smokeless breath, her jewelled eye closed.

And her fire tear fell.

9

Other than when he'd been hunting with the men, Ren had only ever seen one animal die. A mutt so old it had buzzers laying eggs in its matted fur and legs so bent they wobbled when it walked. He was a boy of just six winters then, and life and death were still a mystery to him. Where did the 'life' go when something died, he wondered? He'd asked the mutt's keeper that very question: *Was that what the dead eyes were staring at, the life drifting to its next dwelling place?* The keeper, none other than the gruff Varl Rednose, had bellowed with laughter and flashed his knife in a gouging motion. He had asked Ren if he'd like an eye to stew? Ren had said no. He didn't understand why Varl had found the question funny. The tribe prayed for help from the Fathers all the time and some of them had been dead *for ever*. Surely their 'lives' must be floating over the settlement somewhere?

That day in the cave, Ren learned something about the death of skalers. For one thing, their eyes didn't stare like a mutt's. As the mother's tear struck the floor of the cavern, every rock around it shone like gold, including those where Ren was standing. Her life filled his like rising water. His body grew light and his mind touched the stars. He felt the presence of something extraordinary. It moved around him and through him and somehow *between* him, blowing like a wind from another world. Perhaps the strangest thing of all was what happened to the darkeye horn he still carried. It was lying in a pocket close to Ren's heart. Later, when he would think to look at his robe, he would find a scorch mark on the cloth around the pocket and remember a burning sensation there. But that was later and this was now.

The mother's eye closed and Ren heard the erth breathe as if to welcome her home again. He shook himself alert. He was still in great danger. Rocks were falling. The erth was dancing. The sleeping mountain was no less angry. The skaler in his arms gave a pining cry. Ren stroked it and said a short prayer for the one still minded by the mother's tail, then started for the tunnel.

In his bid to rescue the skaler he had jumped a fair way down into the cavern. Going back up would be a far stiffer challenge. The mountain had been kind to him, though. A number of boulders were heaped in a stack just under the tunnel entrance. Ren bounded over three, then had to stop. A wall of rock now stood in his way. He could rest his hands on the ledge without stretching, and would normally have scrabbled straight up it and away – but not with a skaler clinging to his chest. At best it might fall. More likely be squashed.

'We climb!' he said, aware that his words were stiffer than usual. But how did one talk to a baby skaler? He pulled it off his robe. It took several attempts; as one foot cleared, the other reattached.

Grracck, it skriked, looking frightened and lost.

No time to worry about that. Ren lifted it onto the ledge, forgetting that from there it could see its mother. He watched it turning circles with its wings outstretched, all the while calling mournfully to her. For a moment, Ren thought it would be kinder to leave it. But even as the idea entered his mind the mother's voice was in his head again. *Galan aug scieth*. He pressed his hands to his eyes. What had she *done* to him?

Another shuddering movement underfoot reminded him survival was of primary concern. In one push, he scrabbled onto the ledge. The youngster called again, with a little less hope in its gravelly voice. Ren scooped it up and ran, relieved to see the tunnel wasn't blocked by rubble. He pushed the beast in as far as he could, then dropped to his belly and started to crawl. The skaler, not surprisingly, was frightened by the dark and unsure of what to do.

'Go!' Ren snapped.

The youngster wailed and flapped. But after a couple of head butts and a squirt of dung that landed in Ren's hair, it got the idea and skittered on ahead. Ren spoke to it all the way, but was in the cave before he saw it again. He had a moment of panic when he thought he'd lost it and another when he trod on something soft in the gloom. Horrified, he knelt down and patted the rock. Feathers. Old feathers that crumpled to dust. A beak. A wrinkled leg and claws. He'd stood on a caarker, dried and long dead. Sighing with relief, he pushed the carcase aside but stuffed the foot into his robe. A Kaal hunter wasted nothing. And to string a caarker's claws around the neck was lucky.

By now his eyes were seeing shapes in the rock, but the youngster was absent still. 'Pupp?' he called, using a name he liked, one his father had given to a mutt they'd once owned. With a rustle of wings the skaler found him. Ren bent down and picked it off his ankle. As he tilted his head, a trail of the wet dung fell from his hair and Ren instinctively wiped a hand through it. Strangely, it didn't burn too badly, though the smell was just as raw. He supposed that was because the skaler was young, and probably still to eat meat. 'Galan aug scieth,' he whispered to it. 'What does this mean?'

Grracck, it said again, and nibbled his finger.

Ren pulled his hand clear of the mouth. The teeth, though small, were sharper than grit. To have come this far and be a skaler's first meal would be a cruel outcome indeed.

A draught of cold air rolled through the cave, carrying the cry of an adult skaler. The youngster turned its head and gave a mystified skrike. Ren immediately clamped its jaws shut. It took the full wrap of his hand to do it; the little beast was strong for its size. It responded by pinching his chest with its claws. 'No!' Ren hissed, pulling it away. He raised it up until their eyes were in line. The pupp's were glowing with a pale blue tint, making better use of the light than his. He loosened his fingers to allow it some air. A row of holes along its neck made a wheezing sound. Ren pointed to the far end of the cave. 'They will hurt Ren if they hear you,' he whispered. What gesture said 'hurt' without pain? He opened his mouth and made a quiet 'agh'. The youngster mimicked him (as best it could). Ren sighed and looked toward the light. That call had raised a fresh round of dread. The skalers must be out like a hunting pack. If they saw him with the pupp they would ask no questions, they would simply kill. All he could do – or hope to do – was leave it outside, then hide until nightfall, assuming the mountain didn't take him first, though its rage, for now, had largely blown out.

Folding down the pupp's wings, he crept quietly forward. Never had a light been less inviting or shadows more difficult to find. But the task itself was simple enough: get as near to the outside as possible, wait until the skies were clear, then put the skaler out on the mountainside. They would see it soon enough (or more likely hear it), and the job was done.

The first part was easy. In the wall at the very brink of the opening was a natural recess, deep enough to take Ren and the pupp. He got there just as a skaler flew past. He pressed himself into the shadows, holding tight to the youngster so it wouldn't flap. Breathing slowly, he closed his eyes. Ten breaths later there was still no hint of wings outside and the youngster had settled quietly in his hands. All he had to do was step into the open, stand near to the edge and release the pupp.

But as he rehearsed the action in his mind, his thoughts lit up with more pictures of the mother and her dazzling eyes. What did she *want* of him? Why did this feel like a terrible betrayal when all he was doing was giving the skaler back to those who could care for it?

He broke cover and ran for the light. It was almost the end of them both. The rocks at the brink of the cleft were smooth and weathered, but unevenly layered, eager to trip a careless foot. Ren stumbled to his knees, opening his hands as much to save himself from falling as to let the skaler go. Its wings paddled the air but made no flight. It hit the slope with an awkward splat, slid down on a gaggle of stones and pitched forward onto its back. The noise it made was unbearable, such an indignant squeal that Ren was tempted to bound down the mountainside and immediately retrieve it, as though it had all been a terrible mistake. But the air was trembling to the pulse of wings and a shadow had just swept over the hill. Ren scrambled back into the cleft and made himself as thin as possible. The pupp – still out in the open – squealed fearfully and not without reason. A huge skaler had just come down to land.

It was so close it ate up most of Ren's light. Moving nothing but his eyes, Ren tried to see it. It stretched its sinewy neck and a ripple of colour ran down its scales. *Green*, Ren thought, but then most of them were, darkening a little towards the head. He stilled his breathing, expecting that he wouldn't need to hold the air for long. All the adult had to do was pick up the youngster and fly it to safety. Ren's heart wrenched at the thought. He'd cradled the thing for less time than it took to scratch his rear and yet...

He let his chest down and filled it again. Outside, the big skaler was doing the same, moving the air like approaching thunder. A clatter of rocks suggested it was struggling to hold its position. Ren risked another look, pulling back quickly as the skaler turned its head. It seemed to be scanning the sky for some reason. Why? What was it waiting for? What help did it need to lift up anything as small as Pupp? And why hadn't it made a call to the others to say the youngster was alive and found?

The reason soon became chillingly clear. One of the beast's short limbs came into view. Set among its claws was a large stone.

'No,' Ren mouthed.

Too late. The skaler thumped down with so much force that the rocks zinged and sparks flew. Ren could not believe what he was seeing. The adult snorted, apparently in annoyance, opened its jaws and raised the stone again.

This time, Ren screamed openly, 'NO!'

By rights, it should have been the last word he spoke. But at the very moment he'd opened his mouth another skaler had skriked in the distance, drowning him out. The skaler on the ground gave a worried start. It dropped the stone and replied with a kind of irritated grate. It shook its head as if to say there was nothing to be found.

Then it glanced down quickly, bared its teeth and disappeared into the sky.

10

Stunned. That was how Ren felt. Stunned and hollow inside. After some moments of indecision, he started to make up positive reasons for what he'd just seen. He told himself that the skaler might have been striking at a slitherer that had wound by looking for an easy meal. Maybe the beast had used a rock because the pupp was too close to survive a burst of flame? For all Ren knew, it was, in fact, rescued; when the adult had flown, its feet had been hidden from view. But his mind refused to accept those reasons, and when he at last peered over the ledge there was no sign of any splattered slitherer, just a flash of blue between the stones. The pupp was buried on the slope, not moving. Struck down by one of its own.

Sorrow the like of which he'd never known began to

squeeze Ren's youthful heart. Yet even with the evidence bare before him, he was struggling to believe what had just happened. He ran the scene through his mind once more. Skaler, landing. Pause. Stone. Whichever way he sifted it, the facts came back to him swathed in darkness. A green skaler had cruelly attacked the pupp. It had struck with a stone and…

…not completed the kill!

Ren dropped to a crouch and squinted. Yes, there was a definite twitch of a foot, a little knock of pebble against pebble. Dismissing any thought for his own safety, he quickly jumped down and separated the stones. Amazingly, the pupp was alive, nestled in a cavity between two boulders. Ren remembered the adult's snort of annoyance and wondered if the young one had seen the blow coming and dived into the hole to protect itself. The impact had probably knocked it senseless, giving the attacker cause to believe it had done enough – but also leaving room for doubt.

Carefully, Ren dragged the youngster clear. It was bleeding from a gash where the legs joined the belly. The goo trickled warmly over Ren's wrist, the same green fluid he'd seen oozing out of the mother's head. In that moment, the pupp snapped back to life, kicking in terror and biting Ren's hand. Stifling a cry, he clamped

112

its mouth shut. Grimacing, he looked at the back of his hand. Blood was springing from an arc of fine holes.

A fresh call from the far side of the mountain reminded him of how much danger he was in. The skaler could return at any moment to finish off what it had started.

What to do?

The cave was the obvious answer, but... He wiped his wrist – and that gave him an idea. A slim chance, but it might just work, though it would mean inflicting more hurt on the pupp. 'Forgive me,' he whispered. Kneeling down, he clamped its mouth again and squeezed its belly till more green spurted out of the cut, enough to make a pool on the face of a boulder. The youngster wriggled and jerked like fury, but in a moment it was done and Ren was upright again. He launched the pupp in the direction of the cave, praying it wouldn't crash and hurt itself further. But it was learning fast what its body could do. Instinctively, it beat its fragile wings, this time creating enough momentum to fly a short way and land safely on the ledge.

Ren knelt again. His left hand was burning with pain from the bite, but he ignored it and used the palm of the other to smear the green blood in a trail across the rocks. To this he added some dung from his hair, still wet enough to spread. In a moment of inspiration, he reached into his robe and pulled out the caarker leg he'd found. It was the size of the pupp's, but with one toe less. He planted it carefully at the head of the trail, leaving just one toe showing. Then, with a wary eye on the sky, he pushed as many stones as he could toward the site to try to create the illusion of a rock fall, even managing to tip up a huge boulder before he scrambled back into the mountain.

He found the pupp there, huddled and miserable. This time when he picked it up it didn't struggle, but just settled in his arms as if it no longer cared what happened to it. Ren cradled it in a fold of his robe, then slipped back into the shadows and waited.

Before long, the large skaler came back. It went through all the same motions as before: pausing, breathing, checking the sky. It bent its head and Ren heard it sniffing. He prayed it wouldn't rake the rocks, and it didn't, an outcome aided by a closing shudder from the sleeping mountain that added a last trickle of stones to the pile.

But the skaler wasn't done. It raised itself up and thumped down on the erth with colossal power, doing this twice before it flew off. When all was quiet, Ren emerged from the cave and looked at the site. His 'burial' mound was flattened. Whichever skaler had committed the strike didn't just want the youngster dead – it wanted it deader than dead. For the first time, Ren felt truly afraid. His mission had taken on a whole new twist. He could not abandon the youngster now, nor could he risk another try at returning it. He looked across the silent landscape. The Kaal settlement seemed very far away. Perhaps he should have listened to Targen the Old and never let himself become entangled with the skalers. For whichever way his life turned now, he was going to encounter more enemies than friends, the worst of them being a dark green skaler with a speck of red in its hateful eye.

And a broken fang on its upper left side.

11

Ren decided not to wait for nightfall. The death of the female skaler had brought others to the mountain from all directions. But as time went by and flurries of snow began to drift into the cleft, the sky emptied and he guessed that the beasts had gathered around the great ice lake. If they were anything like the men of his tribe they would have come together to decide what must be done. Now and then he could hear them roaring. He almost felt he ought to be among them, sharing their loss, giving word of what he'd seen. But that was a fever talking. His bitten hand was beginning to swell and purple blotches were spreading out around the tooth marks. He could feel the pupp's fire flowing up his arm, breaking in beads of hot sweat across his brow. Another reason to get home soon. He needed herbs. He needed Targen the Old.

But first he had to attend to their wounds. The youngster's cut was healing quickly. The blood loss, in fact, had almost stopped. Ren spat on his hand and rubbed some wet into the wound, then tied another strip of his mother's under-robe around the belly, knotting it off at the back, between the wings. It was a struggle. Although the little one was yet to grow scales, there were bristles all over its bony body that wanted to stand up at different angles. And like any young animal, it pecked at the binding as soon as it was on. Ren sighed, knowing he had done all he could.

For himself, he made another binding, which he wrapped three times around his injured hand and attempted to tie off using his teeth. While he was labouring, he noticed the skaler sniffing at the dressing he'd applied to his knee. He batted it aside before it could rasp the red stain on the cloth. 'Nuh,' he grunted, the tie between his teeth. He didn't want a skaler tasting his blood. Who knew where that might lead?

Grracck, said the pupp, which seemed to be its response to everything.

Ren went back to his hand.

The pupp, looking on, tilted its snout and tottered forward again, this time stretching its wiry neck and nipping at the knot that held the knee tie in place.

The dressing slipped down Ren's shin.

'No!' he said, and tried to swipe the pupp again, but was overcome by a sudden bout of dizziness, a sway so strong it turned him onto his side. He lay there panting, the mouth of the cave growing large and small. Once again the pupp came forward, lifting its dark wings, sniffing for blood. Ren tried to kick out, but the fever wouldn't have it. This was it, he thought. His life was over. The skaler had numbed him with a poisoned bite. Now he was just a lump of meat, as useless as the caarker he had trampled in the tunnel, as dead as the mutt with its staring eye. Killed by a skaler barely out of its egg.

It was going to eat him alive.

When he woke, the pupp was the first thing he saw.

There was blood, *red* blood, around its mouth.

Horrified, Ren sat up and felt for his knee. He feared he would find the leg severed in half or at best put his fingers in a gory hole. But the limb was good and the wound clean, all its shredded edges sealed. At first he thought it had healed itself and the skaler had grazed on a crust of dried blood. But a gouge like that took days to mend. And though he couldn't know how long he'd been sleeping, he felt sure that very little time had passed. That must mean the skaler had healed him. And all he had done for it in return was to slap it around the cave.

He put out a hand, palm upraised. The skaler was hesitant, but eventually climbed on and seemed glad to be cradled back at Ren's chest. It had pulled off its dressing, but its bleeding had stopped.

Ren tickled two tiny stumps on its head.

Grracck! said the pupp.

Ren laughed quietly. 'Grracck,' he whispered, in a tone he hoped would sound grateful. He glanced outside. The snow was falling steadily now. Not the best conditions for running, but at least he felt better, stronger for the sleep. And though his bandaged hand was still a worry (unlike his knee, it hadn't stopped hurting) now was the time to leave.

With the pupp in his arms, he approached the cave mouth. Another low rumble drifted over the hills. The skalers were still by the lake. What was going to happen, he wondered, when he walked into the settlement and laid the pupp at the feet of Targen? The Kaal might kill the youngster just as gladly as the adult skaler would. But men had voices he knew and understood. Men, he could reason with – he hoped.

First, he had to survive the journey. 'We go,' he said to the pupp. He pointed to the hills, the forest, the scorch line. 'You stay close to Ren.' He made claws with his fingers to demonstrate.

The skaler gurgled and gripped the robe. Ren accepted the pinching this time, but the noises, he knew, would have to stop. He put a finger to his lips and made a shushing sound. The pupp made a happy hurring noise. 'No,' Ren whispered, shushing again. He wagged his finger. The pupp tried to nip it, thinking they were playing. Ren sighed and patted its head. Hopefully, it would get the idea as they went, otherwise one of them, at least, was dead.

All the while keeping a watch on the skies, he took the drop one boulder at a time, careful not to stand on any rocks heavily wetted by snow. If a bone broke now or a muscle tore, the journey home was over before it had begun.

He started to run as he hit the slope proper, the skaler bobbing freely at his chest. The ground chattered as he knocked the shale aside. Noisy, but a risk worth taking, just to get across the scorch line as fast as he could.

He ran at an even downhill pace, covering the ground twice as quickly as he had in the night. The Whispering

Forest was his first objective. Before long, it rose in the distance, a huge ribbon of green flowing over the hills, just starting to be capped by snow. Ren ran and ran, finding rushes of energy he never knew he had. He was almost on the point of self-congratulation, close enough to the trees to think that the skalers were not as smart as Targen claimed, when the pupp made a warning noise. Ren hit the ground fast, pulling up his legs and sheltering the youngster in the curve of his body. The land outside the forest was more green than grey, with few rocky outcrops of any size. Even huddled in a ball, he was going to stand out. And maybe his nose had gotten used to the smell, but his robe no longer reeked of filth. Ren pressed his eyes shut, trembling from his hair to his aching feet. He could hear wingbeats. Close. Very close. Any moment now the erth would boom and a skaler would surely set itself down. All Ren could do was offer up the pupp and the darkeye horn still tucked into his robe and hope that the monster was merciful.

But there was no boom. No shake of the erth. Ren felt the rush as the thing swept over. It was flying low, and yet it had missed him. He took a chance and opened one eye. A skaler was disappearing into the distance. It was one of the two he'd seen fighting earlier. Not the glorious white one tipped with yellow. The other. The strikingly-coloured blue.

He let it fade from his sight before he stood up. A poor (or stupid) hunter it might be, but if nothing else Ren was grateful for the rest. He waved it goodbye, arrogantly thinking he could now afford to stroll into the forest. But as he turned toward the trees, he found his way blocked by the point of a spear.

It jabbed at his belly like the end of the mother skaler's tail, carried by a man no wider than the bones his skin stretched over. A man with so much hair around his face that his eyes looked like two eggs in a nest. Despite the cold, his chest was bare, the skin grown over with dark green moss, notably on his shoulders and back. Twigs and old leaves were clinging to the moss and even some wild flowers sprouted there. A treeman. The first Ren had ever seen. Two more of them rose from the ground as if they had floated up from the grave. The Kaal had always believed that the skalers had driven these men from the forest. Yet here were three, all wielding spears.

'What got?' said the first, dribbling into his beard. His milky eyes squinted at the shape in Ren's hands.

Ren wrapped his arms round the pupp. He wouldn't be able to shield it for long. 'Mutt,' he said.

The treeman squinted. Outside the forest, their sight

was poor. 'Show,' he grunted. He jabbed again.

Ren shook his head. 'I am Kaal,' he said proudly. He nodded at the lowland beyond the forest. 'I have no quarrel with treemen. Let me go.'

A second man stepped forward, the point of his spear less lenient than his friend's. Without warning, he stabbed Ren's bandaged hand.

Ren cried out and the skaler echoed. Its head wriggled free and it hissed like a slitherer. Tiny though it was, its teeth, when it set its jaws wide, were chilling.

All three treemen backed off in fear.

Ren clasped his injured hand. 'Stand away,' he growled, the words burning angrily on his tongue. And at first he thought they were going to allow it, but they looked at each other and seemed to reach a mutual conclusion.

Kill the boy.

Kill the beast.

They came for him, spears raised, murder in their eyes.

A strange sensation flooded through Ren. In the face of this danger he suddenly felt the mother skaler's presence, as if she had emerged from within him like a spirit. But what could she do? He had nowhere to run and no weapon with which to defend himself.

Or did he?

Faster than the treemen could have thought possible, he went into his robe and pulled out the darkeye horn. He held it high in his fist, the way they held their spears against him. Now the mother skaler came alive in Ren. His chest seemed to double in size. The fingers on his bitten hand curled like claws. More remarkable than that, his lips rolled back and he heard himself roar. But it was not the roar the treemen ran from, it was the fire that burst from the darkeye horn. Ren felt it coming like a rush of hot blood, from the centre of his chest all the way down his arm. It leapt across the space between them, catching the nearest man and setting his brittle grey hair alight. He screamed. His spear hit the ground. He fled with the others, beating his face, leaving cinders trailing on the wind. He ran from the boy who made fire in his hand. The boy who could roar like a skaler.

Ren sank to his knees and let go of Pupp. The youngster, who seemed unaffected by the conflict, was happy to potter and graze for a moment. Ren looked at the horn, still glowing at its tip. He clamped his fist even tighter around it, curling his fingers into its spirals. 'What am I?' he whispered. He raised up his hand and stared at the bite marks. The mother skaler had left him now, but during the time she had spent in his mind, she had opened a pathway to understanding, beginning with the words she had spoken in the cavern: *galan aug scieth.* 'I am you and you are me.' That was what it meant. Somehow, she had made herself part of him.

And Ren was coming to know her too, and all that glittered in her haunting eye. She was called Grystina, of the Astrian line. To her son she had also given a name: Gariffred, meaning 'flame of truth'.

Gariffred. On Ren's tongue, it was hard to say. Begging respect, he chose to stick with Pupp. But there were other words that caught his imagination. He had always wondered how they named themselves, these astonishing creatures of fire. Now, with the mother's help, he knew. They hailed from a world they called Ki:mera. And they were not beasts, nor monsters, nor skalers, but went by a word that spilled off the tongue like a storm of fire.

Dragons.

They called themselves dragons.

Part Three

Grendel
and
Graymere

12

'Herbs?' said Gossana, twisting her snout in a way that Grymric found uncomfortable to watch. He had served many matrials in his time spent studying the healing arts, but never one quite as off-putting as Gossana. Those eyes, as changeable as the planet's skies. And those sharpened sawfin scales that somehow felt like an extra set of claws she might use to slash through an old dragon's neck. She had Veng in her bloodline somewhere, he was sure of it. He shook himself and put the thought from his mind.

'The myss has suffered a great trauma,' he said, squinting sideways at the female wearling huddled up at the mouth of the cave. She looked miserable. Worse than that, cold.

'Herbs?' Gossana repeated, as if she expected a great

deal more from the healing dragon than *vegetation*.

'Yes, indeed,' said Grymric, sweeping his claws over the rich array of samples he'd collected, all of them sitting in separate piles, well out of the wind. 'The planet has an endless supply of green forms. I have still to discover what benefits many of them could have for us, but I'm certain that with a little time I can—'

'I don't have time,' Gossana cut in, flexing her glistening claws. 'I need something to raise her out of her melancholy. I was thinking of fhosforent.' She snorted across the cave floor, making the nearest leaf pile dance. They resettled in a less than perfect heap. Grymric shuffled forward and tidied them again, being careful not to show any hint of displeasure.

'I would not advise it,' he said. 'The properties of fhosforent are still unclear and it has never been tested in one so young. In her present state, even the smallest quantity might kill her.'

He thought he saw Gossana raise an eye ridge, but did not care to interpret its meaning. 'Of course,' he said, before she could carp, 'no amount of plant life could replace the warmth of a mother's love – which only a matrial as experienced as yourself could offer.'

Gossana snorted again. Her jaws were tightly clenched, but there was just enough movement in the

130

skin around her mouth to show off her impressive fangs. Grymric noticed she was dribbling slightly and wondered if it would be impolite to ask if she was having a problem with her teeth.

'She's not *mine*,' Gossana growled. 'And she does not want to be. I cannot raise a wearling that will not bond, not even with the noble G'vard at my side.'

These last few words were spoken with a high degree of irritation, leading Grymric to fear even more for the wearling. What hope did the orphan have if its appointed mother did not wish to raise it? And if there was no fondness between that mother and the dragon destined to be her companion, what then?

Thankfully, he didn't have to offer up a comment. At that moment, another dragon appeared in the cave mouth. Grymric was pleased to see it was Grendel, a female he had a great liking for. She took a keen interest in the healing arts and often came to spend time with him.

'Oh, forgive me,' Grendel said, bowing to the superior female. She threw a worried glance at the wearling. 'I did not know you had a consultation with Grymric. I will leave.'

'No...wait,' Gossana said. That glance from Grendel to the youngster had not escaped the old queen's attention. In a silky voice most uncommon to her she said, 'Grymric and I were just discussing the welfare of the orphan. As I think you noticed, she is not what one would want to see in a dragon so young.'

'No,' said Grendel. She lifted her tail and ran her isoscele down the wearling's back. The youngster shuddered and gave out a pitiful, but not ungrateful *graark*.

Grendel looked up to see both adults watching her. Despite the wet trail running from her jaw, Gossana's expression was as close to smiling as any dragon ever came. Grymric, however, had tightened his eye ridges. Displaying signs of affection to a wearling bound to another female might confuse it. He'd expected better of Grendel.

She read his eyes and tented her wings in apology. 'Something my mother used to do for me.' To satisfy Grymric, she pulled her tail well away from the youngster.

But Gossana, who ought to have been the one doing the scolding, stretched her head toward Grendel and said, 'You may be able to help.'

'Me?' Grendel looked puzzled.

And Grymric seemed alarmed. 'In what way might Grendel help?'

Gossana took a breath that bowed her chest and

made her dark green scales clatter. 'How goes your courting, *plentyn?*'

Grymric almost choked on a ball of his smoke. He looked again at his pile of herbs, wondering if Gossana had accidentally ingested an overdose of the green stalks he knew to cause dreaminess. *Plentyn?* Why was she using the ancient tongue? To call a younger female 'child' was a sign of immense fondness – a quality no dragon would ever have assigned to the most fearsome matrial the Wearle had known.

Grendel bowed in acceptance of the compliment. 'I...it is only five days since...'

'Since the Prime instructed you to enter a laying cycle,' Gossana reminded her. 'And no male has come to you yet? I find that hard to imagine.'

Grendel floundered again, her neck scales flushing a light shade of green. 'I...no,' she said.

'But you're so...*radiant,*' Gossana remarked.

Another extraordinary compliment, but Grymric had heard a hiss beneath the words and realised Gossana had slavered her way through them. There was definitely something wrong with her teeth. He broke in nervously.

'The matrial knows that Grendel is entitled to take her time before allowing males to court her.'

Gossana turned and stared him down. The amber eye

(the 'kind one', as some dragons called it) was suddenly glowing as red as the other, sending its sharp light around the cave. 'Don't ever tell me what I *know*,' she growled. 'Grendel's eyes are as bright as new snow. And I see fresh lytes along her tail. Her heartbeats can be heard all around the mountains. Any day now she'll start to *sing*. She is ready. And yet no males pursue her. And she comes here seeking advice from a healer? This can only mean one thing.' She turned and looked at Grendel again. 'She has already made her choice of companion and is actively avoiding all other approaches.'

'No, no,' said Grymric, flashing his tail. Now he did feel able to disagree. 'Grendel cannot choose one male above all others. That would be absurd. I would expect at least four males to be presenting the Elders with their right to do battle to be her guardian.'

Gossana raised her head so high it almost touched the ceiling of the cave. 'Have I suddenly become a vapor? Did I or did I not just say don't teach me what I *know*.'

'Matrial, I...' Grymric shrank into a huddle, his protests now as parched as his herbs.

'Tell him,' Gossana snapped at Grendel, her menacing eyes changing colour again. 'Tell him before I roast his ears. Tell him how your second heart beats for one

134

dragon. Tell him what *colour* that dragon is.'

'Blue,' Grendel admitted weakly. She looked at the sky as if to remind herself.

'Hear that, healer? She desires a blue.'

'A BLUE?' said Grymric, coughing up a long-dead cinder. There were only two blues he could bring to mind: Goodle, who had an excellent bloodline but was a little immature to court a dragon like Grendel, and... 'Not G— Not Abrial?'

Grendel rolled her upper lip.

'I saw the signs during Galarhade's address,' Gossana said, raking one foot with the claws of the other. A web of saliva fell from her jaw. 'Our future queen was making glances at a dragon who is now little more than a renegade.'

'That's unfair and you know it,' Grendel said, her voice approaching the pitch of a roar. The sound boomed around the walls, alarming the wearling and causing her to flap. Grendel immediately corrected herself and leant nearer to the youngster, blowing warm air along her back to soothe her. 'I don't believe Gabrial killed Grystina. I know him. We grew up together. He's gentle.'

Gossana snorted again. 'Not a quality most queens would want in their companion.'

Grymric interceded with a heavy sigh. 'This is not

good. Not good at all.' He was pacing back and forth now, swishing his tail. 'The Elders will not allow this match.'

'Indeed they will not,' Gossana agreed, and yet there was a strangely triumphant tone floating just under her words. 'That leaves us very few options.'

'Us?' said Grendel, growling again.

'Would you put aside my help?' Gossana said. 'Oh yes, the healer has his potions, but he does not understand the hearts of a queen. With Grystina gone, who else can advise you?'

'I do not want your help,' said Grendel, causing Grymric to jump in again.

He stood between them. 'What does Gossana propose?'

The old queen flexed her neck, easing the tired muscles in her shoulders. 'How do you live in this cramped little hole?' Grymric started to answer, but Gossana waved an arm to say the question did not require a response. 'Grendel has two choices, both of which will anger Prime Galarhade. Either she persists in this folly and calls the blue to her, which will bring shame on her bloodline and cause others to question Galarhade's decision to let her be courted, or she allows me to speak to the Elders on her behalf so that the issue might be...resolved.'

'Resolved?' said Grendel, her nostrils widening. She pushed forward a little as if she'd like to bite off Gossana's head. She looked at Grymric. The fine scales above his eyes were almost cracking.

'Love is a complex emotion,' said Gossana, before the healer could speak again. 'If a female admits her affinity for a male, rather than wait for the strongest to fight for her, the process is hard to reverse. For the good of the Wearle, Grendel's liking for…Abrial' – she lashed her tongue around the name as though to flick away a sour taste – 'should not be denied—'

'But he's virtually an exile,' Grymric said. 'How—?'

'I haven't *finished*,' Gossana snorted.

Grymric shuffled back again, glad, for once, of the comforting shadows his 'cramped hole' offered.

Gossana picked up her thread. 'But neither should the match be encouraged at this stage. If the blue should demonstrate his worthiness again, Grendel could yet accept him – though he would be forced to fight for her, of course, once other dragons declare their interest.'

'But who knows how long that might take?' said Grymric. 'Grendel has entered her laying cycle. It could be damaging to her if the feelings she embraces are not played out.'

'Yes,' said Gossana, still irked that Grymric was telling

her her business, 'but it is an outcome easily prevented. It is not too late for Grendel's feelings to be…diverted.'

'*Diverted?*' said the healer. 'What do you mean?'

'She means to give up the myss,' said Grendel, beginning to understand where this was leading. 'She wants *me* to foster the wearling for her, so that Gossana might be free to be a queen again.'

'She…? You…? Exchange places?' Grymric shook his head so hard that his stigs looked in danger of falling off. 'Oh, no, no, no, no, no. That cannot happen. The Prime has made his decision. He—'

'I will speak to Galarhade,' Gossana cut in. 'I will tell him that Grendel had already developed feelings for the blue *before* the quake that shook Mount Vargos, but was too overcome with grief and confusion to inform the Elders at that time. I will add that she has struggled to alter her affections and has wisely sought my advice. We, that is Grymric and I, having discussed the matter further and noted the fondness Grendel has for the orphan, are agreed that she, in her present state, should foster the myss – with my ongoing support, of course.'

Grendel sighed and looked down at the youngster. It had started to rain and the wearmyss was making no attempt to avoid the drops. 'This is most irregular,' Grymric was saying, but Grendel was already

138

speaking over him. 'She's right, Grymric. The wearling will die if she doesn't bond soon with an appointed guardian. Grystina was my cousin and friend. I could raise the myss.'

'Excellent. Then it's settled,' Gossana said.

'Hold your claws,' said Grendel, staring her down. The old matrial rustled her wings. The look in Grendel's eyes was not far short of a call to combat. 'There is still the question of my honour. Before I can formally accept your terms, I must be sure of the Elders' approval.'

'And you will have it,' said Gossana, not quailing in the slightest. 'I will fly to Prime Galarhade's settle directly. You will have your decision before the moon rises.'

'Wait!' cried Grymric.

'What NOW?' snapped the matrial, in no mood to be impeded again. She already had her wings half lifted.

Grymric glanced at his precious herbs, but could not find the courage to ask Gossana to walk to the cave edge before taking flight. Instead he said timidly, 'Your mouth. You're ailing, I think.'

'Pff! It's nothing,' the matrial said. 'I broke a fang on the back of a catch I was hunting. Trust me, its bones fared worse than mine.'

She bared her teeth. For a dragon of her age, her

139

teeth were good, blackened but almost entirely intact – apart from one fang on the upper left side, sheared to a slant and as jagged as ice, stained with the red blood of her prey, and the faintest hint of dragon green.

13

There was no hope for the herb array. One flap of Gossana's wings sent the piles into a spiralling cloud. They seemed to take as long to drop as every leaf in the nearby forest.

The healer sank to his haunches and sighed.

'Don't worry. I'll help you,' Grendel said, already beginning to pick off the leaves that had settled on her scales. 'Now Gossana has what she wants, she won't disturb you again.'

Grymric gave a grateful nod and began the long process of sorting the herbs into appropriate piles. After a while, he said, 'I hope she remembers to speak with G'vard. This arrangement is going to anger him, Grendel. The white has pledged to be a guardian to the myss. If the Elders accept Gossana's proposal, G'vard will be forced to protect a female who sides with a dragon who has caused him pain. Wars have been fought over less. You must go softly around him.'

She nodded, but raised her head proudly and said, 'G'vard must think of the Wearle before he thinks of his pain. If he accepts this arrangement nobly, he will still have a little of Grystina to fight for.'

'I hope so,' said Grymric, his eyes heavy with concern. 'It is vital that a wearling imprints on the father as much as the mother. If G'vard has lingering doubts about his role, it will affect the wearling's character development. The same applies to you, of course. You cannot allow your feelings for Abrial to confuse the myss. This is a brave commitment, Grendel. Some might even say rash.'

'Your words are kindly noted,' she said. 'There is one thing we can be certain of, Grymric. If the myss is not cared for, what hope does she have? Did Gossana say if she had learned her name?'

Grymric shook his head. 'I doubt Gossana spoke to it more than she needed to. Grystina may have died before she chose a name anyway. A queen-elect will usually wait until she knows who the father will be, then names her young accordingly. You knew Grystina well. Given the unusual nature of this family, I doubt G'vard would object if you gave the myss a name sympathetic to her mother's lineage.'

Grendel glanced at the youngster again. The wearling had at last moved out of the rain. Not only that, it was staring at something on the wall of the cave. 'Grymric, what's she looking at?'

'Um?' The healer turned his head. 'Oh, the marks. They're nothing. They were left by the Hom. They make poor i:mages of themselves on rock. You'll find similar likenesses in most of the caves around Vargos.'

Grendel put down her herbs and went to see. On the wall, just as Grymric had said, were some scratchy outlines of Hom figures. They were grasping weapons and chasing an animal. She glanced down at the myss, who was tilting her head and mewing quietly. Grendel circled her tail. With her isoscele, she pointed at the tallest figure. 'This?' she asked. She had picked out the fiercest-looking of the Hom, thinking the wearling might be frightened by it.

The wearling made a graarking sound and brought her tail around as well. She had no triangular scale at the end, just a stub where the isoscele would soon begin to grow. But she could point, and point she did – at a figure without a spear. A figure half the size of the hunting men.

'This one?' said Grendel, moving her tail alongside the youngster's.

'Gffrd,' the wearmyss said, though what actually came out was little more than a grunt. Although dragons learned to speak at an early age, it took them a while to form the most guttural words correctly.

Grendel was certain all the same that the wearling was trying to tell her something. She called Grymric over and repeated the sound to him.

'Guffred?' he said, fleshing it out with a vowel or two.

'Gffrd,' the wearling repeated.

'It sounds like a name,' the healer muttered, 'but—'

'Gariffred,' Grendel murmured suddenly, her gaze drifting slowly into space. 'Grystina was from the Astrian line. She spoke fondly about her great-great-father, an Elder called…' She dipped her head towards the young one again. 'GARIFFRED,' she repeated firmly.

'Graark,' said the wearling, almost falling over as she tried to touch the wall.

'I don't understand what you're getting at,' said Grymric.

But a light was shining in Grendel's eyes. 'Don't you see? It *is* a name. Grystina must have named the drake after her ancestor.'

'No, not *that* name,' Grymric said, smoke balls puffing out of his ears.

'Why not?'

'Because… Oh, you know your history,' he spluttered. 'Why would Grystina burden her drake by calling it "flame of truth"? No one can prove that the Astrian line was closer to Godith than any other dynasty. That argument was settled before I was born, with a great deal of bloodshed, so I was taught. To bring a drake called Gariffred into the Wearle would be a direct snub to Prime Galarhade's authority. And Elder Givnay would not approve on spiritual grounds, not to mention the fact that his family is long connected to that conflict. Why would Grystina, that most sensible of dragons, wish to cause any hint of controversy? These are tense times, Grendel. Do not speak of this, I beg you. It will only make matters worse. Besides, the drake is dead. Its name is of little consequence now.'

But Grendel wasn't done, and her next words fell like icy rain around Grymric's ears. 'I disagree. I think she's trying to tell us what happened to her brother.'

'*What?*' the healer exclaimed. Had Grendel lost all grasp of her senses? He had herbs for that kind of malady, he thought – if only he could find them.

'We must summon the Elders without delay,' she said.

'Why don't you speak to me instead?'

The imposing figure of G'vard had suddenly filled the cave mouth. Despite her surprise, Grendel found herself impressed by his stealth. He had glided silently into the cave and closed his wings without disturbing a single herb. She wondered how much he had heard.

Grymric, who looked grateful for the break in proceedings, said, 'Ah. Perhaps I should leave you two… three to get better acquaint—'

'Stay where you are,' G'vard growled. He looked harshly at Grendel and nodded at the little one. 'Is it true?'

'If you mean about the wearmyss, yes.' She manoeuvred herself to stand over the wearling.

G'vard pushed his thick neck forward, the muscles hardening all along its length. 'How dare you make an arrangement like this without consulting me or—'

'I didn't,' Grendel cut in fearlessly. 'It was Gossana's idea. Show her your impressive teeth, if you must. The future of this wearling is all that matters. You will do as you pledged and protect us.'

'Her,' G'vard thundered, stabbing his tail at the terrified youngster. 'I pledged to protect *her*. Not you.

Not the consort of a traitor.'

'Gabrial did not harm Grystina,' she growled.

G'vard whipped his tail back and held it aloft, a sign of his deep displeasure. 'Listen to her,' he snorted at Grymric. 'Hear how she openly defies the Elders.'

'She is…confused,' Grymric offered weakly.

But Grendel stood proud. And boldly she said, 'Gabrial and Grogan are falsely accused. I know. I have proof.' From the corner of her eye she saw Grymric wince.

'PROOF? I was *there*,' G'vard hit back. 'The blue caused an eruption; the whole Wearle knows it.'

'One of the Wearle knows differently,' said Grendel, 'and she was closer to Grystina than you.' She stood aside to reveal the marks on the wall.

For the last time Grymric tried to interrupt. 'Grendel, in the name of Godith, please let this go.'

'No,' said G'vard, flicking out his claws. 'Let's hear the female's "proof".'

The healer winced again, sipping air through his teeth. This was going from bad to dangerous. To use the term 'female' – that is, not to refer to Grendel by name – was a dreadful slur. Even afflicted by anger and grief, it was unlike G'vard to shame another dragon so.

'Look at the wall,' Grendel said plainly.

147

G'vard sharpened his gaze on the figures. 'Hom. What of it?'

'She points to them and says her brother's name.'

Grymric strangled a breath. But Grendel had thankfully not revealed the name.

And G'vard was showing no interest in learning it. He pulled his nostrils tight together, the worst expression of scorn a dragon could make.

'Don't you see? It means they were *there*,' said Grendel.

'Who? Where?' Grymric asked.

'The Hom were at Vargos,' Grendel explained. 'The wearmyss saw them in Grystina's birth cave. That's why she points at the figures.'

G'vard snorted and shook his head wildly. 'If the Hom were at Vargos, Grystina would have burned them, and we would have seen their ash.'

'Well, perhaps just one of them,' Grendel snapped back, floundering around her theory a little. 'A young one. A smaller one, that might hide in a crevice.'

'And not be scented? They are Hom. They *stink!*'

'We must tell the Elders,' Grendel insisted.

'Grendel, listen to me,' Grymric cut in. His tone was firm; he had heard enough. 'The Elders will not believe a wearling's babble, and nothing will bring Grystina back.'

'But—?'

'No, plentyn. Hear me out. Even if the Hom had escaped our patrols, how could they have caused the eruption we saw? They do not have the power to i:mage such a thing.'

'At last, some words of *sense*,' said G'vard. He moved closer to Grendel, until they were almost snout to snout. 'I am flying to Galarhade right away to withdraw my offer of guardianship. I would rather return to Ki:mera in shame than be an unwilling ally to that idiot *blue*.'

And with that he gave a formal bow and backed out of the cave.

Grymric, glad now to see him go, let out a weighty sigh. 'In the name of all that is noble and good, how can we suffer such dreadful wretchedness? It's this planet, there's something *odd* about it, something that blights a dragon's soul. Did you see G'vard's eyes? Did they seem in any way dull to you? There was something ailing him, I'm sure. And I don't just mean Grystina's death. His condition was akin to a worker I saw at the fhosforent mine this morning. Dullness of eye; quick to anger. When his fire has simmered I must go to him and offer assistance. In the meantime, I pray to Godith to bring down the night before any other vile misfortunes befall us.'

These words were spoken with heartfelt concern, but Grendel was about to land one more blow. Stroking the wearmyss again, she said, 'If I leave her with you, can you feed her, Grymric?'

'I – sorry? Leave her? Here? With me?'

'Just until morning,' Grendel begged. 'Make some i:mages for her. She'll like that.' She produced one, quickly. A star that popped when the little one touched her snout to it.

'But…where are you going?' Grymric asked.

'For help.'

'Help?'

'If my guardian deserts me, I must seek out another.' Grendel bent her head low and spoke softly to the wearling, then raised her head to the healer once more. 'I name her Gayl, after her mother's mother.'

'Yes, yes. Very apt. But where are you *going*?'

'To the edge of the domayne,' Grendel gulped. 'Where the sweepers fly.'

And before Grymric could protest, she had backed up to the cave edge, spread her wings and flown.

14

Halfway across the valley, Grendel could still hear Grymric's cries for her return. But her mind was set. She would follow her second heart and seek out Gabrial. He would believe her if no other dragon would.

The problem was where to look for him. Although she was old enough to roam freely, the mountain domayne was vast and her knowledge of it limited. She had spent most of her Erth time aiding Grystina, seeking out suitable birth locations. It was Grendel, in fact, who'd discovered the opening that led to the cavern in Mount Vargos (a thought that still made her sleep uneasy) and though between them they'd explored large sweeps of the mountains, they had never flown far beyond sight of the sea. She had therefore never seen the fabled scorch line that was supposed to keep the Hom at bay.

But she knew a mapping dragon that had.

It was dark when she landed at the fhosforent mine, but the lytes on her underwings never dimmed and she barely had time to fold down her wings before she was spotted by one of the Veng. It came to her like a long, thin dart, landing so close that she almost lost her footing on one of the sharp gradients that marked the outlying hills around Vargos. She had never thought herself afraid of the Veng, but she had never been challenged by one before. Stilling her primary heart, she raised her head and announced herself.

'I am Grendel, from the line of—'

'I know who you are,' the Veng said bluntly. 'What are you doing here?'

Grendel readjusted her optical triggers. Despite her enhanced night vision, the Veng was little more than a pointed head with dull red eyes, the remainder of its body a wedge of obscurity against the sullen backdrop of the mountain range. 'I am free to go where I please,' she said, doing her best to mask a tremor. She caught herself glancing at the Veng's harsh claws. 'If you stand in my way, Prime Galarhade will know about it.'

The Veng was unimpressed. 'You're not a queen yet,' it snarled, tilting its head as though it wanted to sink its teeth into her throat. 'So I'll ask you again, what are you doing here?'

Now its stigs were bending back as its lip curled clear of its upper fangs. Attack mode. Why? What had she done to incense it so? Yes, the Wearle needed security, but weren't the Veng here to make her feel *safe*? A dragon of this class should be bowing to her, not drawing her into a petty conflict. Grendel blew a wisp of smoke, being careful not to trail it across the Veng's face. All the while, she could feel her third heart shrinking. That tiny compass of spiritual devotion that kept all dragons on the path to Godith was reacting badly to this encounter. Something was wrong here. Something that filled her with a strange sense of dread.

Before she could determine the root of her fear or even start to answer the Veng's question, a second dragon landed beside her. She recognised him as Graymere, one of the De:allus breed, sent to oversee the extraction of the fhosforent. The De:allus were quick of mind and good at solving problems. Some rose to be Elders later in life, though many shied away from that position, preferring instead to devote their lives to the science of interpreting the physical wonders of Godith's universe. Graymere was larger than the Veng and had a striking purple hue throughout. Like all De:allus he had bright yellow eyes, a feature associated with high intelligence. De:allus normally kept their eyes half lidded, because at close range the yellow glare was off-putting. Graymere's lids were fully raised tonight, which meant Grendel could see the Veng clearly in the darkness. Was it her imagination or was it less green than it ought to be?

'Fanon Grendel,' Graymere said, exuding a little air from his spiracles. He spread his wings and bent the tips up. This was a sign of deep respect, probably a little more than Grendel deserved. But she was still, technically, in a laying cycle and any male, even one as committed to his work as Graymere, was entitled to consider himself eligible for courtship. She blushed, the green pallor just visible, thanks to his eyes. It pleased her to hear him use the term *fanon*, a word from the old tongue meaning 'a female yet to have young'.

'De:allus Graymere,' she said, tipping her snout.

He folded his wings. 'May I ask what brings you here?'

Only the slightest portion of his tone carried any hope that she *was* inviting courtship, though Grendel was certain if she took off now he might decide to chase her round the mountains. The De:allus needed to further their lines as much as any other class of dragon – and there was no denying that Graymere was handsome.

'I already asked her,' the Veng said tetchily, its eye ridges narrowing by half.

Grendel raised her head and made another wisp of smoke. 'Does a dragon in my position need to give a reason for exploring the domayne?' She thought this sounded a little lofty, but Graymere's reply was perfectly polite.

'Of course not,' he said.

'Then I would like to see the work you do here.'

He seemed surprised, but bowed nonetheless. 'It would be my pleasure,' he said. The stigs on the back of his head were bristling. 'In fact, this is the perfect moment. We are currently in a resting phase. The workers have retired to their settles – it's a splendid time to see the fhosforent seams. Veng Gazz has no objection, I assume?'

The Veng snapped his wings open, almost slashing Grendel with the fine-toothed spikes that ran along their edge. 'I have better things to do than watch a fawning De:allus embarrass himself in front of a female.' With a *whump* that pulled in a raft of cold rain, he banked sideways and slipped away into the darkness.

'My apologies,' Graymere said, when Gazz was

gone. 'I am forced by Elder Grynt to employ the Veng's services. No dragon is comfortable around them, I assure you.'

'Is he well?' asked Grendel. 'Only, his scales seemed dull. And he was hostile, even for one of their class.'

Graymere peered after Gazz, into the darkness. Choosing his words with care, he said, 'You must keep this to yourself, but I would not be surprised if Gazz was taking a supply of fhosforent, and possibly encouraging other Veng to do the same.'

'Taking? You mean *stealing*?' Grendel said.

The De:allus rustled his wings, a gesture that suggested she should keep her voice low.

She apologised and leant a little nearer to him. 'Have you reported this to Elder Grynt?'

Graymere fanged his lip – something he seemed to make a habit of, judging by the scrapes and scars around his mouth. He too did not look in the best of health. But any dragon tasked with managing the mine and dealing with the angry attentions of the Veng could be forgiven a few skin lesions, Grendel thought.

He said, 'Fhosforent begins to degrade almost as soon as it's removed from the rocks. It's hard to keep a record of how much we've mined. I would need to be certain a crime had been committed before I dared inform Elder Grynt of my suspicions. The consequence of falsely accusing a Veng is too alarming a prospect to consider.'

'Then how will you ever prove his guilt?'

'You saw him,' Graymere whispered. 'If he's stealing the ore, he's eating it.'

'But wouldn't that strengthen him? I thought fhosforent improved our fire?'

'In small amounts, yes,' Graymere agreed. 'But it's hard to know how much Gazz has eaten. The darkening of his scales is deeply puzzling – even Veng Commander Gallen has commented on it. But it's not his loss of colour that concerns me, more the change in his temperament.'

'Fhosforent affects his mood?' said Grendel.

The De:allus nodded. 'Most of the combustible minerals we ingest improve our fire through chemical reactions, a mechanism that has evolved over countless generations – forgive me if I sound like I'm tutoring you.'

'No, please, go on,' Grendel said.

'Fhosforent works by expanding the fire sacs, giving us the power to eject more flame, more quickly. To be safe from harm, the strength of flame we're able to discharge must never overwhelm the tissues that protect the lining of the throat. The heat of a fhosforent flame can quickly wear those tissues down, thus exposing the organs of the brain to a pressure they would not normally accommodate.'

Grendel blinked her soft blue eyes. 'You mean, it's driving him mad?'

Graymere fanged his lip again. 'Too early to say. But if Gazz's behaviour becomes any more erratic, he will be his own ruin.'

Grendel nodded. Now she understood where that sense of dread in her third heart was coming from. She looked at Graymere and felt sorry for him. No one could blame him for not wanting to speak to the Elders about Gazz. But why was this even happening? Dragons stealing? On Ki:mera, such a thing would be unthinkable.

'So, the mine,' the De:allus said, raising his neck to show off his fine array of purple shades. 'It's not only fhosforent we dig for, of course. One of the benefits of being on this world is that it offers many interesting rock forms to graze.'

'Really?' Grendel said doubtfully. 'What I take from the gravel heaps all tastes the same.' She was referring to the piles of loose stone that were stored in places close to the eyries. These days, it was considered distasteful to see Elders gnawing at a rock face for the essential minerals all dragons needed. On Erth, the mine supplied stone chips for all.

'Most of it is,' Graymere said, nodding. 'A basic grit is all that's required to aid the digestion of raw food and give us what supplements we need. If you're interested, I could show you a range of the different substrates we've mined and talk you through their properties?'

'I think I'd prefer to see the fhosforent,' said Grendel, trying to sound as graceful as she could. She admired Graymere's passion for his work, but one rock was much like any other to her.

He angled himself toward the mountains. 'The best are on the external slopes. Why don't I chase— I mean, fly you over our latest find? It will be lit by the moon. It's quite impressive.'

'I'd like that,' Grendel said. 'The workers – you said they were resting now?'

'Yes, until morning – well, except one.'

Grendel lifted an eye ridge.

'Rogan,' he said.

Grendel steadied her breathing. Rogan was the real reason she was here. 'He works in the night?'

'His own choice,' sighed Graymere. 'The Veng push him hard, but he is allowed rest time – he simply will not take it.'

'But…he's old. He must be exhausted?'

Graymere nodded, clearly not at ease with the situation. 'Dying of exhaustion, I'd say. He speaks in strange sentences, a never-ending babble of incoherence. He's an excellent worker. He has already uncovered two promising seams, but is always keen to dig harder and deeper; his talons, I'm told, are worn to nothing. He is a poor sight, Grendel. Have no fear, I will make sure we fly well clear of him.'

'No,' she said, before Graymere could launch. 'I want to see him.'

The De:allus blinked his yellow eyes. 'Why?'

'He knew my father.' (It was a distant connection, but it wasn't a lie.) 'If Rogan is ailing as badly as you say, I want to see him – alone – and offer him forgiveness. This is my right as a queen-elect.'

'But if Gallen finds out I've taken you to—'

'This will rest between you and me,' said Grendel. She stretched her beautiful wings, casting a soft light all around her. 'Now, show me fhosforent glowing in the moonlight. I cannot think of anything more appealing, can you?'

And then it was Graymere's turn to blush. 'Follow me,' he said. And with a rush of pleasure lifting his wings, he took off into the night.

15

It was indeed an impressive sight. On an ordinary night it would have been impossible to see any natural features in the mountainside. But where the moon shed its subdued light against the slopes, the rocks sparkled in frills and patches, just as if the sky had spilled its stars upon them.

Using his eyes to light the way, Graymere strafed the scarps and ridges, ending his tour with a jet of flame that made a small portion of the ground explode, showering pink sparks high into the sky.

Grendel was breathless with wonder by the time Graymere invited her to land on a bluff above a quarry filled with misshapen rocks. They were some way from Vargos now, cresting a narrow range of hills that wrinkled in a long tail back to Skytouch.

'Did that please you?' he asked.

'It did,' she confessed, her lytes glowing brightly. 'The sights – and the guide.' She kept her words pleasant and true, but without suggesting anything deeper – though the heat from her neck could not be denied. Had her second heart not beat for Gabrial, she would have been more than happy, she thought, to bring up wearlings in Graymere's company. But Gabrial was the one, she was certain of it. To be sure of deflecting their dialogue away from anything that might be misleading, she said, 'Was that fhosforent you burned? I thought you didn't allow that?'

'An impure seam,' he said. 'The finest crystals are deep in the rock. By burning off the layers of a weak or scattered seam, we can sometimes reveal a stronger vein underneath. We have lost a few good sources that way, but it spares the talons of the dragons who work here. Grymric spends a lot of time healing claws.'

Grendel nodded. She'd been scratching at the rock face as she listened to this. Although a dragon could crack a large stone between its claws, endlessly gouging the surface of a mountain had to be painful and damaging over time. 'Is there no other way to retrieve the ore?'

'Not as yet,' Graymere answered truthfully. 'Patient

grazing still serves us best. We alternate the workers and rest them well. They're young, so their claws regenerate quickly. Some prefer biting to gouging. Regrowth keeps the incisors healthy.' He showed her his two most prominent teeth. They looked sharp enough to slit a clean edge through cloud. 'Dragons that work the mine will boast of a fighting advantage over others. A myth, in my opinion, but we're never short of volunteers. Recently, we've been testing ways of opening a seam by i:maging fissures in the weakest strata.'

'You mean, Prime Galarhade works the mine?'

A faint splutter of smoke left Graymere's snout, hiding him for a moment in a yellow haze. 'Forgive me,' he coughed, 'I don't wish to belittle you. I understand why you would think that. Prime Galarhade does have extraordinary powers of physical i:maging, but, no, he does not attend the mine. Elder Givnay is helping us.'

Grendel's eye ridges tightened slightly, a not unpleasant look on her. 'I thought Elder Givnay hardly ever left his settle?'

'He doesn't need to. We map out the mountainsides and i:mage him any promising sites. He does the rest remotely.'

Grendel dropped her jaw in disbelief. Elder Givnay could i:mage *remotely*? She knew his mental powers

163

were legendary, but to mine rocks from a distance was astonishing.

Graymere went on, 'I pray the technique is perfected soon, if only to spare dragons like Rogan more trauma.' He nodded at the void. 'You'll find him down there. Listen for the scraping and the sounds of his voice. I can light the first part of your descent from here. Call if you need assistance.'

'Thank you,' Grendel said. She tented her wings and pushed away from the ridge, needing nothing more than the night air to glide on. Under Graymere's light she was able to gyre down without clipping the sides of the quarry. But as the drop increased and the light grew less, she looked around for a suitable perch and landed safely on a smooth cold boulder, close to the centre of the pit.

She opened her ear ducts fully. Right away she heard Rogan's voice. He was singing quietly, like a wearling might. A song about a fire star that opened in the heart; a gentle cry of unrequited love from an elderly dragon who had never been a father as far as she knew. It touched her deeply to hear it. Tonight, she decided, someone would share his lament.

She began to join in, harmonising softly as she clambered nearer to the sound of his voice. He faltered when he heard her and she thought at first he might stop and hide. But as her notes drifted sweetly through the darkness, he picked up again. He was still singing as she reached his shoulder.

'Per Grogan?' she said, ignoring Galarhade's ruling on the name. What did it matter down here? 'I am Grendel, of the Fissian line. You knew my father. Will you speak with me?'

He could see her, she knew, for the moon had moved well clear of the clouds, giving their eyes sufficient light to work with. He continued singing as if she wasn't there.

She tried again. 'I have flown here from Skytouch. I need your help.'

'Be gone, vapor,' he croaked.

Was that what he thought she was, a spirit? 'I am no vapor,' she said, looking at the rock he was working. It was streaked with dark green blood. To her horror, his claws had completely worn away, his arms little more than infected stumps. He was using bone to dig for the ore.

'Per Grogan, please stop this,' she said.

She reached out to him. A bad mistake. He turned on her and roared, but didn't use flame. She backed away, her primary heart pounding. Graymere would have heard that. Another burst would bring him to investigate. Or worse, bring Gazz.

'I wish you no harm,' Grendel said urgently. 'Please, you must help me.'

This sounded callous in the circumstances, but she had seen his eyes when he'd challenged her. They were void of colour, their once-jewelled surfaces cracked and dull. He was going to die in this pit and he probably didn't care. There was little Grendel could do for him, but still much he could do for her.

'I am charged with caring for Grystina's wearmyss. I believe I can prove that you and Gabrial were not responsible for the quake at Vargos.'

'Varrrrgos,' he slurred. He punched the rock, cracking a splinter of bone.

It was all Grendel could do not to empty her gut. She fought back a dangerous tear. 'Brave dragon, I want you to sleep with the knowledge that you and Gabrial were true to the Elders. But first, I must find him. You were a mapper once. One of the best in the Wearle. You know the domayne like no other dragon. To which region of the line would they send him, Grogan? Where will I find the blue?'

He moaned and swept his head back and forth, babbling in the manner Graymere had described, some unrelated murmurings about his mother, then a complicated chatter about rock locations. Even now, punished by madness, he was using his mapping skills to chart the position of every stone in the quarry.

'Gabrial… ?' she pushed him.

He twitched and seemed to have a moment of lucidity. 'I know no dragon of that name,' he growled. Then he was muttering again and moving away to a new location.

'Please,' she said, scrambling after him. 'Gabrial – Abrial, whatever you want to call him – is the only dragon who can help me. There were Hom in the mountain when Grystina died. *Hom*, Grogan. You have been misjudged. I want to see your honour restored. In the name of Godith, please help me find Gabrial.'

'Godith,' he murmured. And he swayed for a moment, gathering himself, before emitting a roar that shook the whole pit.

Grendel instinctively spread her wings. In the darkness, the rumble of rocks was terrifying. Their hewn cries wailed like the spirits of the dead as they cleaved and slid and bounced over one another in their quest to find their lowest resting place. She immediately took off, hovering at a level just above the jumble. A fearful madness had taken hold of Rogan. He was snarling and biting and thrashing his tail, calling Gabrial's name in challenge. At the place where he'd been scraping, a pink seam winked like an open wound. Rogan set his jaws against it, and using what remained of his shattered teeth, he grated raw fhosforent into his mouth.

He was seeing Gabrial in every dragon now. And as the pink ore melted and his fire sacs enlarged, he unlatched his jaw and tried to burn Grendel. The result was horrifying. A bright red flame poured out of his throat but quickly billowed back around his head, setting him alight down the length of his neck and all along the edges of his wings. At the same time, his body was going through a terrifying change. He seemed to be withering, turning black.

Grendel screamed and flapped away, helped by the warm air rising from his body. Graymere was flying to her aid by then, but he was rapidly overtaken by two of the Veng. Gallen, the Veng leader, was in the air as well. As he swooped overhead he gave a command that would haunt Grendel for the rest of her days.

'Kill it,' he hissed.

And the Veng burned, without mercy, what was left of the dragon that had once been Grogan. They aimed their fire at his open mouth, forcing it deep into his broken body until the flames had vaporised the tissues within and he exploded in a fizzing ball of scales. They had taken him down as if he were nothing but hunted prey. Just a *thing*, consumed by hatred and darkness.

No longer a dragon at all.

16

'Give me one good reason,' Elder Grynt said angrily, as rain began to fall in steady lines around him, 'why I should not send you back to Ki:mera to spend the rest of your days teaching wearlings how to scrape *dung* off their tails?'

'I was roaming, as I'm free to do,' said Grendel. She proudly lifted her head, taking the opportunity to swivel one eye and glance at Gallen. The Veng commander was behind her, pacing back and forth through puddles forming in hollows in the rocks.

'Look at me!' Grynt thundered. The dark tints in his purple face were more prominent than Grendel had ever seen them. She looked at him squarely, fearful of the power in his brilliant green eyes. 'You went to see Rogan the traitor,' he said.

'Elder, may I speak?'

'No,' Grynt snarled at the healing dragon. Grymric, along with De:allus Graymere, had been summoned to Grynt's superior eyrie – a high ledge on an isolated slope. Green hills and a strip of forest one way, Vargos and the open sea the other. Grendel had been brought here during the night and guarded till sunrise by two of the Veng. As if that wasn't serious enough, Elder Givnay was also present. Givnay had silently impressed upon her the need to open her third heart fully. Godith was everywhere and nowhere, he'd said. No harm would befall her if she spoke the truth.

Grymric bowed submissively and shuffled back.

'You went to Rogan,' Elder Grynt repeated, water dripping off the wavy stigs that grew beneath his chin. 'Why?'

'To offer comfort. He was cruelly mistreated by your Veng.'

'He mistreated himself,' Gallen cut in. 'And when I got there, he was shouting the name of the blue. Now why would he do that?'

'Well?' said Grynt, smoke winding from his nostrils.

Grendel looked away. 'Gabrial was his charge—'

'Abrial,' the Elder reminded her. 'Dishonour the name of Godith once more and you *will* be

171

removed from the Wearle.'

Grendel sighed and bent her knee. She glanced at Elder Givnay for support. The spiritual leader of the Wearle was sitting with his foreclaws pressed together, his eyes focused on the shape they were making rather than on Grendel's anxious face. She said, 'Rogan was…confused.'

'And so are you,' Grynt said, 'if you think you can lie to me any longer. Do not forget you are in the presence of Elder Givnay. One word from me and he will enter your mind and scrape the truth out. I know about your arrangement with Gossana. I know about your *feelings* for the blue. The only reason you would go to a mapper is to check on layouts or ask for directions. The healing dragon has testified to me that you intended to seek the blue's help. Why?'

'I tried to stop her,' Grymric said weakly.

'Silence,' snapped Gallen.

Grynt continued, 'Answer my question. What were you planning to do if you found the sweeper?'

Grendel was shaking. The rain was drumming hard on her back, as if it would have the truth from her too. She might as well tell it, even though they would mock her. 'I believe the Hom were in Vargos when Grystina died.'

'What?' said Graymere, as if he'd suddenly woken

172

from sleep. He stepped forward, shaking water off his wings. The whole eyrie grew a little brighter, thanks to the widening light from his eyes. 'What's this about the Hom?'

And so Grendel told about the wearmyss, Gayl, and the drawings they'd seen in Grymric's cave, including her suggestion that the Hom were somehow to blame for the quake. The healer, she noticed, was shaking his head. But Elder Givnay was looking at her carefully now, as if he'd like to float into her mind and view the evidence for himself.

De:allus Graymere spoke up again. 'This is extraordinary,' he gasped. 'Has any of it been reported to the Prime?'

Gallen snorted in amusement. 'You expect the Prime dragon to believe the ramblings of a *wearmyss?*'

'She spoke her brother's name,' Grendel said fiercely.

'So?' said the Veng.

'So he might be alive,' Graymere said breathlessly, all the while keeping his gaze on Grynt. 'You heard G'vard's words at the funeral: he couldn't say for certain what happened to the drake. What if Grendel is right and the Hom got in and took the wearling? What if he's out there, beyond the scorch line?'

'Impossible,' sneered Gallen.

Turning on him, Graymere said, 'What would it take to send out patrols over all the Hom settlements? Or are you so unsure of your questionable security that you're too embarrassed to go looking for one so young?'

'Freeze your fire,' spat Gallen, flicking out his claws. In the rain, he looked even more hostile than usual. 'You may be quick of mind, but I could have those yellow eyes on my tongue before you'd have a chance to blink them again.'

'Enough,' Grynt rumbled. His gaze fell on Graymere. 'You are forgetting, De:allus, that our "questionable security" rests ultimately with me. There will be no patrols.'

Graymere hung his head, as though to let his frustration drain away. 'With respect, Prime Galarhade should know of this.'

'And he will,' said Grynt, 'when I have a mind to amuse him with it. The death of Rogan has angered and distressed him. The Prime is resting.'

'Is he ill?' said Grymric, his concern feeding into his jittery eye ridges.

'No worse than this De:allus,' Gallen muttered.

Graymere ignored the slur and said, 'When the news of Rogan's death begins to spread there will be great unrest among the Wearle. Thanks to Gallen's brave *defenders*, Rogan died without shedding his fire tear. You don't need the brains of a De:allus to know what mutterings *that* will cause. The Veng that summoned me here were already talking about the Tywyll.'

'The Tywyll?' said Grendel, looking shocked. As a wearling, she had heard many frightening tales about the fabled black dragon without a third heart, but she had never expected to encounter it. She turned to Grynt, whose jaw was set rigid.

Graymere said quietly, 'If the roamers believe that a black dragon has risen among them, there will be panic. News that Grystina's drake could be alive will do much to ease any superstitious whispers. I'm sure Elder Givnay sees the wisdom of that?'

Givnay lifted the tip of his tail and slowly turned his isoscele, a gesture that could be taken one of two ways: he was either intrigued or irritated. But as no thoughts were flowing from his mind, it was impossible, just then, to say which.

Graymere went on. 'Prime Galarhade should be informed of this – now. The longer we wait—'

'I have *spoken*,' Grynt said, in a tone so deep it wafted the rain aside momentarily. 'Grendel has beguiled you with her stories, De:allus. Next you will want me to believe that the Hom have captured the first Wearle and are hiding them somewhere among the trees.'

'But—?'

'I have spoken,' Grynt snapped again. A rivulet of water ran between his eyes. 'I will not tolerate another interruption. The Wearle will be told that Elder Givnay is praying for the auma of Rogan and asking Godith to accept his fire. Any talk of black dragons will immediately be quashed.'

'And the Hom? The drake?'

'Forget about the Hom. They are no threat to us. I do not believe they were in the birth cave or that they caused the quake. You have already told me that Rogan disturbed many rocks in the mine. Is this not further proof of his guilt?'

Graymere fanged his lip. He wanted to say that any dragon with a loud-enough roar could disturb a small amount of quarry rock, but not on the scale they'd seen that day at Vargos. He sighed for Grendel. Her case was hopeless. Without real proof of the Hom's involvement, the blame was always going to fall on Abrial and Rogan.

The Elder turned to Grendel again. 'Would I be right in thinking you planned to ask the blue to search for the drake?'

A run of air rippled the length of her neck. She nodded.

'You know that is treason?'

Grendel gulped in alarm. 'But...I was acting in the interests of the Wearle.'

'That is *my* job. Yours is to breed and tend to wearlings. I asked you at the start of this dialogue for one good reason why you should not be sent back to Ki:mera in shame, and I ask you the same thing now. Be careful how you answer.'

'Gayl,' she said meekly, lowering her head.

'Correct,' he said. 'You will return to the myss and raise her well. On behalf of the Elders I am prepared to accept that your second heart misled you and that this folly with the blue is nothing but a youthful aberration. But I warn you, any more of these disturbances and the Fissian line will fall into disgrace and the myss will be left to run wild. Is that what you want?'

'No.'

'Then you are dismissed – no, wait, I have one more thing to say.'

Grendel looked away from him, trying not to frown. What more humiliation could he burden her with?

The Elder raised his chin, showing off his fine array of silver breast scales. 'G'vard has come to us asking to withdraw his offer of guardianship.'

Grendel sighed. 'He will...admit his duty and

come around,' she muttered.

'He will not,' said Grynt, racking up his tongue. 'G'vard is a noble dragon who through no fault of his own has been placed in an adverse situation. I am therefore willing to grant his request and put another candidate in his place.'

'Who?' said Grendel. She looked up in time to see the Elder's hard gaze drift toward Graymere.

'Me?' the De:allus said.

Veng Gallen snorted in amusement. 'Did you hear that, Elder? I never knew it was possible to hear a dragon *squawk.*'

'You deny there is affinity between you?' said Grynt.

Graymere flashed a look at Grendel. She was staring into space, her jaws wide open.

A blush of green ran the length of Graymere's neck. The rising heat in his scales turned the drying rain to steam. 'There is some affinity, yes, but—'

'Then it is done. This is my ruling.'

'But...the mine? Who will oversee the fhosforent? The workers?'

'The Veng will take full control,' said Grynt.

'The *Veng?*' Graymere rose up as if he'd been stabbed by Gallen's claws.

'The order comes from the Prime,' said Grynt. 'More

178

lapses of security will not be tolerated.'

'There was no lapse of security,' said Graymere. 'And if there was, Gallen should look first at his own wyng.'

The Veng commander bared his fangs. 'Meaning?'

Graymere ignored him and spoke closely to Grynt. 'This is wrong. The mine should be closed. We must investigate the pit where Rogan was working. Something unnatural happened to him. He was going through some kind of change when he died. Grymric and I should examine his remains and—'

'You are relieved of your duties,' Grynt said impatiently. 'Unless you want to take Rogan's place?'

Graymere inhaled sharply. He looked at Grymric, hoping he'd find some support from the healer. Grymric shook his head. This was not the time to argue, he was saying.

'You are dismissed,' Grynt said to Graymere. 'I hope you and Fanon Grendel have pleasant days together. Elder Givnay will bless the union.'

Givnay, dutifully, bowed his head.

Graymere locked his teeth together, bringing some purple back into his neck.

The rain continued to fall in lines.

And Grendel finally closed her mouth.

17

Words. They had never seemed so strange or so difficult before. Every time Grendel tried to converse, her sentences trailed away into the rain. Graymere's, likewise, when he spoke to her. All that made sense in their first few moments were the hurrs and grunts of the wearmyss, Gayl, destined now to be the focus of their lives.

Shortly after being dismissed by the Elders, Grendel had retrieved Gayl from Grymric's cave and flown her directly to Graymere's settle, an open crag just behind the mines. Despite the range and scope of the mountains, there were few available caves around Vargos, certainly none that could shelter three dragons. The rain was of no concern to an adult; they enjoyed the pulse of it on their wings, and a concentrated fall of water would wash out the parasites that lodged between their scales. But a youngster could become severely wet. And though Gayl was unlikely to die of exposure, it was nevertheless preferable to keep her dry until her first layer of scales came through.

So Graymere found himself saying, 'I should roam. Find shelter. For her, for…us. She cannot sit under you all the time. I have heard there are caves further out. Shall I…?'

'Yes,' Grendel said, knowing they would be better apart for a while. 'Go to the mine as well. There must be arrangements you need to make?'

He nodded and bumbled through a reply. 'The mine. Yes. Arrangements. Yes.' He tented his wings and prepared to fly. 'Grendel?'

'Later,' she said, her voice full of kindness, 'when you've found shelter for us.'

He fanged his lip. 'I will…care for you,' he said. He looked down at Gayl, curled up in a ball between Grendel's legs. 'Both of you.'

'*Hurr*,' went the youngster, tucking her snout under her skinny tail.

'And we for you,' said Grendel, meeting his gaze. Even half lidded, his eyes were so sad. 'Go. We will wait until you summon us.'

He nodded again, and bowed. 'Keep her safe,' he said, and flew.

There was no activity at the mine, though Graymere had been expecting that. Heavy rain could dilute the freshly-exposed ore or simply wash it out of the seams. The workers would be on their settles, resting. It hurt to think that his work here was done. They'd been his, this desolate group of hills. His project. His reason for leaving Ki:mera. He was proud to be a guardian, albeit by command, but fostering was not his true vocation. He was De:allus, born to unravel the mysteries of the universe, born to understand the wonders of Godith. He was going to miss these harsh grey scarps, and the hollows and shafts his dragons had dug to find and retrieve the precious pink ore.

Ah yes, the ore. Perhaps a life of fatherhood was better for him now. How could he ever look at fhosforent again without reliving Rogan's horrifying end? What was Rogan thinking of when he'd swallowed so much of the pink, so fast? Did he know what effect it would have on his fire? Or had something turned his mind before that? Like a gathering storm, these thoughts began to pull his gaze toward the quarry, and before he knew it he was flying there. What he was looking for, he couldn't say, but a chance to investigate might never come again.

To his surprise, the pit was not deserted. One of the workers, a good-natured green called Gruder, was almost on the spot where Rogan had burned. He was sniffing at the stones and racking them aside, his head bent low to the ground.

Graymere landed with a quiet clap of wings.

'De:allus Graymere,' the green said, jumping around. He looked nervous. Or distressed. Possibly both. Rain was bouncing off the top of his head, making spikes as tall as his primary stigs.

'Gruder, what are you doing?'

The young dragon made clamping movements with his mouth. 'I…' He put his shoulders back like a guard. 'I was told you were removed from your duties,' he said, as if he had read it off a nearby rock.

Gallen's words in Gruder's mouth. Graymere gave a quick snort of contempt. 'I have been chosen to raise the wearmyss,' he said, making it sound like a great honour, 'but I could hardly leave my position here without…' How could he put it without worrying Gruder into calling the Veng? '…saying a prayer for Rogan.

No matter the reason he was sent to us, none could deny he was an excellent worker. One of our best. Wouldn't you agree?'

Gruder swallowed hard. 'I'm sorry, I must continue with my work.'

'Of course – what has Gallen ordered you to do?'

The young dragon swung his head from side to side, his wings hanging limp like the last leaves on a tree. The rain pounded on the rocks around him as if drawn down by the weight of his fear.

'Gruder, you know me,' Graymere said. 'You are in no danger. None of this will reach the ears of the Veng. Why are you working when the others are at rest?'

'I don't like this,' said Gruder, taut with dismay. 'Godith will punish us. We should not…'

'Not what?' Graymere pushed him gently.

Gruder shuddered, rattling every scale from his neck to his isoscele. 'They want me to find his *heart*.'

Graymere felt the tips of his wings turn to ice. A dragon had three hearts, closely linked, but it was clear to him which one Gruder meant. The primary heart was the organ that supplied a dragon's strength. Its walls were as thick as three layers of scales and almost impossible to pierce. Yet when a dragon died those walls would open and out of them would come a single spark. By a means unknown, even to the finest De:allus minds, the spark would travel to the dragon's eye where it would enter a single tear. With the shedding of the tear, the auma of the dragon was released into the universe and its spirit could be one with Godith once more. But if the death was unnatural and the tear didn't form, the heart would close around the spark and its walls would gradually turn to stone. Then, legend had it, the auma of the dragon would forever haunt those who'd denied it the chance to die in peace. That could arguably include the whole Wearle.

No wonder Gruder was frightened.

The rain eased to a softer beat. Graymere blinked his eyes, clearing the runnels of water that sometimes collected in the folds of his lids. 'You must do your duty,' he told Gruder kindly. 'If your auma is pure, nothing can harm you.'

But the dread in Gruder's eyes did not marry with that statement. 'Is it true?' he whispered. He was shaking like a wearling.

'Is what true?' said Graymere.

'That the Tywyll came for Rogan at the end?'

Was *that* the rumour the Veng were spreading? That the change observed in Rogan was the spirit of evil, risen? Graymere set himself strong. 'No, Gruder, that is not true. I was there. The darkness played no tricks on me. Rogan was distressed, driven mad by…his confinement. He was not in control of his flame. I assure you no dark spirits rose. What is to be done with the heart – if you find it?'

'I am to carry it to Veng commander Gallen.'

'And then?'

'I don't know. The Elder was here. I suppose he will decide.'

'Elder Grynt?'

'No, Elder Givnay visited this morning.'

Graymere narrowed his ridges. Givnay was here? The mute had left his settle – for the mine? 'Have you found anything?'

Gruder blew two lines of smoke, first from one nostril, then the other. He pointed to a piece of ground where a few charred pieces were stacked.

Graymere adjusted his position to bring himself close to the pile.

'De:allus, please,' Gruder said urgently. 'By order of Veng commander Gallen, no dragon is allowed to examine the remains.'

'Did he say why?'

'No. Not to me.'

Graymere gave a thoughtful nod. He raised one foot and let it rest on the remains. 'Pray with me,' he said.

The green twitched nervously, looking all around him.

Graymere said, 'Relax, Gruder. Not even Gallen would deny a blessing on Rogan's spirit.' And he bowed his head and appealed to Godith, asking Her to accept Rogan's auma and take him back into the Fire Eternal. And as Gruder bent his head as well, the De:allus closed his short rear talon around a piece of bone and gripped it neatly under his foot.

Leaving Gruder to continue his work, he flew out of the pit, heading for the settles on the ocean side of the mine. He had almost reached them when he was rudely intercepted by none other than Gallen, who happened to be accompanied by the dragon Graymere had come to find: a talented mapper called Garret.

The Veng commander ordered Graymere to land. Graymere chose a strip of waterlogged erth. Not the ideal place to stand up to a Veng, but the ground underfoot was very soft; he could bury Rogan's bone with one push if he needed to.

'You're out of your territory,' Gallen said bluntly.

Graymere glanced at Garret and back. 'I was seeking Garret, not you.'

'And what would you want with a mapper?' said Gallen.

'I could ask you the same thing,' Graymere said, though the answer was obvious. The Veng prided themselves on knowing every piece of the territories they defended, and Garret was the best mapper in the Wearle.

Gallen spread his claws under Graymere's snout, sending mud in all directions. 'I warned you not to mock me, De:allus. The mines are my business now and I will do all I need to protect them.'

'How might I be of assistance?' said Garret. Like Grymric, he was a gentle soul who did his best to avoid any conflicts. His quiet intervention was enough to make Gallen retract his claws.

'I need to find a cave – for three,' said Graymere.

'Um, yes,' said Garret. 'I heard about your new... appointment. You must be proud to be—'

'Get on with it,' snapped Gallen. 'We've got work to do.'

Garret gave a chastened nod. 'As you know, the atmospheric conditions of this planet have weathered out many fine hollows in the mountains. The best have been claimed by the Elders, of course. There are some spectacular sea caves I could point you to, but they may be too damp for a new-born wearling and the overlying strata can be quite unstable.'

'You're testing my patience, mapper.' Gallen's claws were out again. 'You'll be unstable if you don't answer his query soon.'

'Garret, just show me something safe,' said Graymere. 'All I need is shelter for now.'

So Garret closed his eyes and concentrated. Within moments, he had built a floating i:mage of a wide green hill, topped by a cluster of mature trees. 'We've mapped several formations in this region,' he said, 'where an ancient fault line has divided the land. There was an extensive body of water here once that has worn down the rock and carried loose sediment into the hill. Drainage cracks have expanded all over it and several attractive caverns have formed. The best one is here.' He turned the i:mage to show an undulating slope. In one fold was a dark gash. 'It has ample mineral deposits and three subterranean branches, plus pillars of varying heights. Ideal for a playful wearling. Follow the mountains to their natural end and you can't miss it.'

'It looks exposed,' said Graymere. 'Low to the ground.'

'It's also near the scorch line,' Gallen said, pouring smoke across Graymere's chest. 'Be careful you don't get stolen by the Hom.'

'I can show you others,' Garret offered, feeling a little squashed between the stares.

'Thank you,' the De:allus said quietly. 'I'd like to explore this one – if commander Gallen has no objection?'

'The further away the better,' said Gallen.

And with one more brooding exchange of glances, Graymere recorded the i:mage in his mind and left without another word.

18

Garret was right. The cave was easy to find. The dwindling grey backbone of mountains pointed like a drawn-out isoscele to an unrestricted tract of hills, only one of which had trees at its peak. Graymere swept over it, studying the cave from several angles. It was, as he'd feared, a little low to the ground. Grynt could think what he liked about the Hom, but until the wearling grew, it was vulnerable to attack.

Using his optical triggers he scanned every gap between the trees, registering the scent of any sizeable creature, moving or still. Birds were active in the trees, and on the hill was a plentiful supply of rabbits (a good meal for a growing wearling). Swinging further out, he was pleased to see a pale stream wiggling through the fields, with good vegetation all around it. A few wingbeats

191

beyond the stream, running almost parallel to it, was a long dark streak in the grass: the scorch line. It was the first time Graymere had seen it, and he didn't get long to study it now. His nostrils began to twitch as they picked up the scent of another dragon. It was approaching low with the sun at its back, flying fast and breathing fire. At first he thought it might be Gallen, chasing him down because he'd discovered the theft of Rogan's remains. But it soon became clear that this was not the case. A young blue swept underneath him, renewing the scorch line with bursts of flame that left the ground scored and crackling, blackened.

The blue was good at his job. As soon as his fire sacs emptied, he lifted and banked, then reversed his course and burned the line in the opposite direction. It was on his next run that he noticed Graymere and switched course to join the De:allus in the sky.

'Do I know you?' said Abrial, gliding alongside.

'No,' said Graymere, 'but I know you.'

Abrial tipped his wings and circled. What dragon *didn't* know him by now?

'You were Rogan's charge,' Graymere said, as Abrial passed by on the other side.

'Yes,' the blue said eagerly. 'You have news of him?'

So word hadn't reached the domayne edge yet. This

192

was going to be difficult. 'We should land,' said Graymere, and pitched towards the hill.

Moments later, they were facing one another on the ground. Out of habit, Abrial stood a little lower than the visitor (when reporting to Gallen, he was expected to look up). 'Tell me of Rogan. Is he still at the mine?'

Graymere bent his claws around the remnant, a bony piece of wing, shrivelled and blackened by the heat of the Veng. He kept it out of sight as he spoke. 'I am Graymere. I ran the mine,' he said. But that was as far as their dialogue went. Suddenly both dragons snapped to attention as they heard the sound of a fast-beating heart and smelt the scent of a Hom approaching. Abrial was swift to react. He turned, stood tall and spread his wings – a passive gesture taught by Gallen to scare off anything from small animals to Hom.

But the boy kept coming, using both hands to pull himself up the slope. He was deep inside the scorch line and not stopping. Abrial snarled and filled his fire sacs. He directed a flame above the boy's head. The pressure knocked the Hom a short way down the hill. The boy cried out, more in anger than in fright, but picked himself up and came at them again, shouting something in his feeble Hom voice.

'He's wounded,' muttered Graymere. Wounded and

limping. The boy was stained on his arms and chest with the strange red blood that leaked from his kind.

'Why doesn't he stop?' Abrial said anxiously. By now, his battle stigs were fully extended. 'He must go back. He must know I could kill him?'

'This will send him back,' said Graymere. And he pushed his head forward and bellowed a warning, setting off cries of alarm in every animal to the far horizon.

The boy screamed and clutched his ears. He fell to his knees, writhing and clawing at the sides of his head. Blood ran in trickles through his fingers.

'Nudge him over the line,' said Graymere. 'And make sure he sees your fangs.'

But as Abrial prepared to step forward, the boy spoke a sound that both dragons thought they'd misheard at first. Then he spoke it again, in a slur, before collapsing face down onto the ground.

Abrial felt his claws contracting. He looked at Graymere and Graymere at him. The boy had just mimicked the speech of a dragon. It was thin of tone, but unmistakeably a word.

'*Tada?*' Abrial said.

The De:allus nodded and whispered the translation. Tada: *father*.

Part Four

Ned

19

The Kaal settlement, two days earlier.

Knowing it might be several days before Targen the Old would awaken from his dreams, the body of Utal Stonehand was stripped and washed by the women of the Kaal. He was dressed in a white robe ready for burning, or for taking to the darkeyes' cave. His fate now rested with the wisdom of the Fathers.

By the end of day one, with nothing better to occupy his thoughts, Ned Whitehair began to wonder why he had not heard sound of his son for a while. He asked the boy's mother – Mell – this question as she was walking to the river to wash. 'Seen Ren?'

Mell laughed and shook her tangles of hair. 'Perhaps the growlers have got him at last.' For Ren liked to climb trees and he liked to taunt growlers.

But that was before the skalers had come.

Then Mell stroked Ned's cheek and said, 'I'll be thanking you later for that flower, Ned Whitehair.'

'Flower?' said Ned.

And Mell just smiled and walked on toward the river, wiggling her fingers high in the air as if she knew of something Ned had forgotten.

Ned shook his bemusement aside and continued his search. He spoke with the men. 'My lad, Ren. Seen him lately, makin' bother?'

'No,' said the men, each one.

Mystified, Ned returned to his shelter. He untied the reins on Wind, his white whinney, planning to take his search into the woods. It was while he was swinging his leg across her back that a quiet voice said, 'I knows where Ren Whitehair might'n be.'

Ned looked down. The voice belonged to the girl, Pine Onetooth. A strange child by anyone's measure. She seemed to waft around the settlement like a leaf on the breeze. He stroked Wind's mane. 'Say your piece, girl.'

She pushed her tongue into her lip and pointed at the mountains.

A deep sigh escaped Ned's chest. Skalers. The boy

was obsessed with them. 'When?'

The girl broke a reed of grass in two. 'A night back. See'd him runnin' in the shadows o' the moon.'

A night back? Now the mountains drew a long gaze out of Ned, their snow-tipped peaks mostly hidden in cloud. He thought on Pine's words and began to connect them with something Ren had said at the meeting, something about dung and using it to hide from skalers. 'Sweet mercy of our Fathers,' he said below his breath. He glanced down at Pine again. The girl smiled back as best she could. Ned said, 'Do you watch my boy always?'

'Some,' said Pine, sniffing a flower.

Ned nodded to himself. 'If he should return, you may marry him one day.'

'Mebbe,' said Pine, swaying to the thought.

Ned shook Wind's reins. He made to kick her belly, but stopped. Those words Mell had spoken about the flower itched as badly as the nibblers in his robe. Back when they had courted, he'd given flowers then, often riding high into the steepest mountains to find the pretty blue petals she liked. But he hadn't picked a flower for many a moon, so...?

He climbed down off Wind and strode into the shelter. Sure enough, there was a flower on the skins where Mell laid her head. A chilling fear crept over Ned then. He began to throw the heavy skins aside, looking for something he hoped would be there – but wasn't.

The boy had taken the darkeye horn.

Leaving skins everywhere, Ned ran to Wind and leapt onto her back. The whinney took off as much out of shock as from the smack Ned gave her. He heard voices as he rode – 'Ned, what's the bother?' But Ned put his head low and galloped. He rode Wind all the way to the scorch line, to the place where the hunting party, Ren included, had watched Utal burn.

'REN WHITEHAIR!' he thundered into the mountains. Wind reared above the blackened grass. 'REN WHITEHAIR! I KNOW YOU'RE OUT THERE, BOY! YOU COME BACK TO ME NOW, YOU HEAR!' The words faded into gentle echoes. Ned turned the whinney and trotted her along the right side of the line. 'REN WHITEHAIR, SON OF NED! CALL LOUD TO YOUR FATHER AND YOU WON'T GET A BEATING!'

Nothing. Ned cursed and gritted his teeth. In truth, he had never once beaten Ren, but crushing him with relief might not be out of the question this day. He turned the whinney and trotted her the other way. 'REN! WHITE! HAIR!' No response. Ned looked at the skies. Empty. The same could not be said of his gut, which felt as though it were lined with stone. 'Mell, forgive me,' he whispered, and galloped Wind across the line.

As he rode, many thoughts screamed through his mind. There was no point trying to track the boy. If Ren had done as he'd boasted and used the dung to cover his scent, Ned could be searching until he grew old; the plains were covered in skaler waste. Most likely the lad had made for the sleeping mountain, where the skalers liked to settle, and anyone familiar with these hills could find hiding places. But why had he taken the darkeye horn? What was the stupid boy planning to *do*?

Whatever the answers to these questions might be, Ned was not about to learn them then. Suddenly the way ahead filled with shadow and a roar like the crack of stone split the sky. Wind pulled herself up and reared. Ned fought to hold her but was thrown before he could steady her head. She fled, leaving him to face the skaler alone. His first instinct was to roll into a ball. But if he was going to die, he would die standing up, though the skaler had its own ideas about that. The first time Ned tried to get to his feet, the beast swooped over so fast and so low that the pressure of air knocked him onto his back. Shielding his face, he looked for the thing. It was gliding in a circle, wings as blue as the cloudless sky, tail flicking to give it momentum. Breathing hard, Ned managed to rise. He spread his arms wide, palms fully open.

'LOOK AT ME, SKALER! I HAVE NO SPEAR! I HAVE NO *FIRE*! ALL I WANT IS MY PRECIOUS BOY!' He turned with it as it circled again. 'MY BOY!' Ned screamed. He levelled one hand to the height of Ren's head.

But the skaler showed no sign of understanding. It swooped again, quicker than Ned could judge, and out of its mouth came a ball of flame that seemed to consume every morsel of air. Ned reeled back clutching his throat, gagging as the suffocating heat swept over him. It pulled at his robe and sucked at his innards. The centres of his eyeballs felt like they could boil. 'My boy,' he managed to say once more, but the fight had gone out of him now and his brain was thumping with two clear choices: raise a fist and lose an arm like Utal, or retreat, rethink, and live to fight again.

He chose the second option.

The skaler watched him all the way to the scorch line, firing out another harsh ball of flame when Ned stumbled wearily across it.

Ned turned and pointed a shaky finger, making sure the blue beast saw him. 'I will remember you,' he panted, 'and in the name of my Fathers and the tribe of the Kaal, I will kill you first if my son has been harmed.'

The beast snorted and swept overhead.

And Ned, his pale skin reddened and blistered, turned and began the walk back to the settlement, two thoughts ringing clear in his mind:

Find the darkeyes.

Kill the skalers.

20

Halfway home Ned was met by two friends: Oak Longarm, younger brother of Utal, and Waylen Treader, a farming man. Both were on their whinneys. Waylen was holding tight to Wind.

Oak dismounted and ran to Ned, catching him in his powerful arms. 'Ned, rest steady. It's me, Oak. We found Wind runnin' free. What's happened?' He clamped Ned's face and raised it up. The skin was peeling in several places. That told Oak what he needed to know, but he asked the question anyway. 'Skalers?'

Ned closed his eyes and nodded.

Oak Longarm shuddered, thinking of his brother laid out in white on a raft thick with spiker branches. 'Water,' he said to Waylen.

Waylen slid off his whinney and took a pouch from a

rope at his hip. He spilled cool water over Ned's face. Ned gripped the pouch and drank in great gulps.

'You crossed the line?' asked Oak.

'Aye,' Ned said, his white hair dripping.

'We see'd you take off on Wind,' said Waylen. He took back the water pouch and drank from it too. 'Why, Ned? What's the bother?'

So Ned told all – about Ren, the flower, the horn, the blue skaler.

Oak Longarm stared at the mountains.

'We must gather the men and search,' said Ned.

Waylen spluttered with laughter, spilling water down his robe. He wiped a hand across his mouth to dry it. 'I fear the beast has nipped you, Ned. How shall we take men across the line? That way brings death on us all.'

'He's my son,' said Ned.

'Aye, an' I have two right similar. Both good lads. Would you send their father to dance in flames 'cos Ren were dull enough to cross the line?'

Ned raged at him for that, but Oak Longarm stood between them, strong.

'Ned, this ain't the way,' he said.

'I'll have his tongue on a stick and his spit to sauce it!'

'If you want yer arms broke, you might try,' said

Waylen. He was a big man with a jaw like rock. The lines of his face were nearly as rough as the fields he ploughed. He shook a flutterfly off his shaggy black hair.

Oak pushed Ned back. He was leaner of face than both his companions and as handsome again as his brother was plain. 'Ned, you know that Waylen speaks fair. Crossin' the black line ain't the way.'

'Then Varl has it right – we must wake the darkeyes.'

'What?' said Oak, pulling back a little.

'If the beasts have killed my boy, let us punish them for Ren and your brother as one.'

'Ned…' Oak sighed and looked away.

Waylen stabbed the toe of his boot into the erth.

Ned threw up his hands. 'Speak loud, friends. I would hear you on this.'

'Targen has given his ruling,' said Oak. 'Utal burns on the water, tomorrow. We are not to seek vengeance against the skalers.'

'No,' Ned wailed, staggering back. He ran his hands through his scorched white hair.

'I like it as little as you,' said Oak. 'But the Fathers have spoken. We cannot go against them.'

'Am I not a father?' Ned beat his chest. 'And you a brother?' He strode forward again and struck Oak's arm with the back of his hand. 'Are we to do nothing to free ourselves from the curse of these beasts?'

'Ned, you must think straight,' Oak said. 'Wait another day. Ren may yet walk clear of these hills, unmarked. We all know he has the luck of the stars upon him. As for my brother, I will weep for him as he flies to the Fathers and that will be enough.'

'For you, aye,' Ned said, coming close. 'But what would Utal have wanted?'

Oak gulped and turned his face away. For all his wise and mindful talk, his eyes were suddenly soft with tears. On gritted teeth he said, 'We cannot slight Targen. My brother has been prepared for burning. We cannot steal him away to the caves.'

Ned nodded. 'I hear you true. But what is to stop us going there without him?'

Waylen pinched his eyes into a frown.

'We three,' Ned said, looking at the farmer. 'Let the darkeyes see my face and know their enemy flies again. Let it be us who claims these mountains back for the Kaal.'

A cool breeze swept between them. Waylen's whinney ruffled its mane. Oak snapped a twig beneath his boot and said, 'The old ones are saying it would be a poor ride. In their chatter they ask why the darkeyes have not yet stirred or how the skalers have failed to find them. What if the darkeyes are gone, Ned? Or fallen dead in their cave? What are two against a host of skalers, anyway?'

Ned stroked Wind's ear and swung onto her back. 'Old men chatter like farts in the wind. If the darkeyes take only one beast down, we will have smiled on your brother's spirit. Now, will you ride with me, or will you sit here and chew on your memories?'

Oak and Waylen exchanged a glance.

'My fields are sown,' said Waylen. ''Tis a dreary day waiting for corn to poke through.'

'For my brother, then,' said Oak, getting onto his whinney. 'My brother and the Kaal.'

And they gripped hands, these three brave men, and turned away from the sleeping mountain toward the valley where the darkeyes lay.

21

They rode long and into the night, stopping where the river narrowed to a pinch to rest a while and water the whinneys. Oak put an arrow through a careless hopper and cooked it over an open fire. The three spoke little and slept until morning, woken by the patter of rain on their camp.

They crossed the river with Waylen leading. On the far bank, the ground rose steeply away from the water and continued to rise before levelling out to a run of green hills, spotted with trees and bald patches of rock. Waylen pointed to the far horizon, where the only hill of substance, a thick-set tor thinning to brown over most of its surface, stood at the end of a shallow dale.

'When the battles were done, that's where darkeyes were tracked to,' he said. He stroked the ears of his whinney as if he sensed it warming to the coming danger.

Ned patted Wind's neck. 'Then that's where we go.'

'Ned, wait,' said Oak, taking hold of his reins. 'My fury for vengeance has brought me this far, but my wits are begging me to stop now and speak.'

'Then say what you will,' Ned replied fairly.

Oak sat high and stared at the hill, pressed from above by grey clouds dark with the threat of rain. 'How are we to raise these creatures? And more so, how will we chase them into battle? We will be their foe the moment they see us. I would rather die in the flames of a skaler than see myself rot from a darkeye's spittle.'

Waylen slanted his gaze Ned's way.

Calmer for his sleep, Ned looked to the skies as if hoping for a sign. And right away, there it was. He pointed to a skaler, some way off. 'We bring a skaler down – as near to the cave as we can.'

'How?' asked Waylen.

Ned laughed. 'By being Kaal. Even this side of the line, the beasts won't bear our taunts for long. The first fire will bring the darkeyes out. Then we have a battle, do we not?'

'Aye,' breathed Oak, as he walked his whinney on.

'And we three best pray to the Fathers we are not caught in the midst of it.'

By midsun they were at the foot of the hill, on the crumbling bank of a near-parched stream still alive with a shimmy or two. Ned fancied he would see the ground strewn with bones or hear the scrubland hissing in pain where the darkeyes had left their poisonous bile. But all was quiet and disturbingly plain. The only animals Ned could see were going about their lives, untroubled.

'Where is it?' said Oak, meaning the cave.

Waylen pointed to a chin of rock. 'On the far side of that.'

Ned scanned the slope they would need to climb. It was stonier than it had looked from a distance, and where grass grew it was heavily tufted. An easy task for a mountain man, but difficult for their rides. He slid off Wind's back. 'We'll leave the whinneys here. They won't find foot on ground so ill. And if we run them on it, we'll likely be thrown. Is there cover, Waylen?'

The farmer leant sideways and spat. 'No.'

Oak dismounted and passed him the reins. 'Wait here, by the water.'

The sun was on Waylen Treader's face, but no words of warmth flowed out of his mouth. 'Don't slight me, friend. I dint make this ride for the pleasure.' He showed Oak the hilt of a knife, tucked firmly into his waist. Like most Kaal, Waylen was a skilful hunter. He could skin a hopper quicker than any man.

'No sense in us all gettin' killed is what I'm sayin'.'

Ned took Oak's side in this. 'You done well, Waylen, leading us in. But Oak's right. We need the whinneys calm and ready. This is our fight: Oak's brother, my boy. If we burn on this hill, someone needs go back and tell it.'

Waylen spat on the ground again. 'I say we're better as three.'

'And I say not,' Ned Whitehair challenged.

And that was an end to it.

Oak pulled a sheaf of arrows from his saddle. 'How high do you think I can aim?'

Ned smiled and slapped his shoulder. 'If any man can prick one, your long arm will.'

With that, the two men crossed the stream and quickly began to breast the hill, picking up a winding, sideways path. For the first time in many a day, Ned was pleased to be climbing again without fear of what was flying overhead. But in his heart he knew he must always

212

be alert. If they strayed too close to the darkeyes' lair, they would face an unpleasant greeting. He remembered the horror on the faces of the Kaal when the darkeye had landed in the midst of the settlement. Skalers, despite their fearful size, were as handsome in their way as any flower in the field; but darkeyes, they were loathsome creatures, drawn from a deep well of evil, to be sure.

'Ned!' Oak suddenly pointed to the sky. A skaler, the one they'd seen earlier, was circling.

Ned instinctively dropped to a crouch. 'It's seen us and it's wonderin',' he whispered. He watched those incredible eyes changing size. He could almost read the curiosity in them.

The beast glided by without making a sound.

Oak snared a breath. 'Did you see it? Did you see its colour? Green, like the one that burned my brother.' He pulled the bow off his back.

Ned stayed his arm. 'Not here. We must be closer to the cave. Come on.'

He took the lead, running uphill at a sensible pace, avoiding as much loose stone as he could. Before long they were flat against the lip of the mound that Waylen had pointed out by the stream. Green hills flowed to the distant horizon. But not far over the rise the ground cut away like a yawning mouth. And barely a stone's throw down was the cave where the darkeyes supposedly slept.

Ned rolled onto his back, panting. In the sky, the skaler had cut its distance by half. 'Get ready,' he whispered. He patted Oak's arm, then scrambled upright and stood on the ridge.

'Skaler!' he shouted, and cursed his stupidity right away. With Oak's arrows at hand, they could have provoked the beast in silence. But all Ned had done was alerted anything with half an ear to the presence of men. He glanced at the cave. No sign of movement. What if Oak was right and the darkeyes were gone? What if the skalers had killed them already? What if this was nothing but dangerous folly?

The skaler sailed over, its green tail glinting in the lazy sun.

Without warning, Oak released an arrow. It whistled off the bowstring, quivering to its target. To Ned's surprise it struck and held, waggling freely in the nick between two of the beast's huge toes. The skaler squealed. Its claws flashed out. The arrow fell to the hillside in silence.

'Sweet mercy, what now?' Oak Longarm said. Neither man had expected to hurt the skaler, merely to annoy it.

'The cave,' said Ned. He extended a hand to help

Oak up, all the while keeping his eye on the beast. The skaler's forward momentum had kept them out of range till now. But it was turning smoothly, setting itself low. It was going to attack.

'The *cave?*' hissed Oak.

'We have no choice,' barked Ned.

He hauled Oak onto the ridge. The beast was still some distance away, but Ned had not forgotten how fast they moved. Sure enough it was on them in a blink, so close he could *feel* the rumble of its roar and breathe the choking stench of its power.

'Down!' he yelled.

They ducked and went sprawling in one movement, helped in their fall by the pressure of heat. A ceiling of flame raged over Ned's body as he tumbled haphazardly toward the cave. He heard Oak cry out and saw him sliding, beating down a small fire at his shoulder. His robe was burned, the flesh underneath it eaten through to the jointed bones. The bow lay broken behind him. Arrows were scattered all over the ground.

'Oak, to me!' Ned screamed.

But the skaler had already turned and there was no ridge this time to hinder its aim. It opened its jaws with a deadly click and Oak Longarm went to the Fathers in a curling flare of orange light. Ned saw his outline briefly, a dancing ghost in the heart of the flame. And then there was nothing but the smell of seared earth and the terror of Ned knowing he was going to be next. His only hope was the cave and a different form of evil. He ran for it, his head full of rage and torment.

Where were they? his mind was screaming.

Where in the name of the Fathers were the darkeyes?

22

In his time, Ned had thought more than once about dying, but he had never imagined it might be like this: trapped far from home in a hole in a hill, waiting for a fire-breathing terror to trace his scent and melt his bones. Survival was a stubborn friend to all men, but as Ned crept along the wall of the cave, feeling his way deeper into the darkness, there seemed little chance it would side with him today.

Unless this place had hidden depths, he was certain now the darkeyes were gone. He tried not to dwell on that wretched thought. Oak Longarm had met with a horrifying end – and all that Ned had gained from it was the hollow discovery that there was no way of fighting the skalers. He cursed his stupidity and his pride. Targen the Old had been wise in his rulings. A life of peace was better than a death spent yearning for vengeance. Now Ned was primed to learn that lesson, in the most brutal way imaginable.

The skaler entered with a bad-tempered snort, extinguishing most of the light. Ned tensed as the beast shuffled forward, loading the air with its lumbering sweat. There was very little room for its giant frame, but how much room did the creature need when its fire was more flexible than any limb? A short, hot flame punctured the darkness. It licked around the cave walls and billowed into nothing. It easily missed Ned, who had pressed himself into a protective nook, but it did briefly light the way ahead. In that instant, Ned made a startling discovery. He'd been wrong about the darkeyes.

They *were* here.

Two of them, hanging from the roof of the cave. They reminded Ned of the strange black flappers that batted around the settlement at night, but these were larger, three times the height of a man. The skaler had seen them too. Its eyes were now radiating light into the gloom – enough to illuminate the darkeyes' shape. Ned braced himself, expecting a bigger gush of flame. But the beast seemed more confused than threatened. It pushed right forward, its long snout passing Ned's hiding place. From the back of its throat came a number of colourful rumbles and clicks, as though it might be trying to communicate. The darkeyes did not stir, but something was moving within the cave, a presence not even Ned was aware of till Waylen leapt onto the skaler's neck, and crying vengeance loud enough to wake the dead, plunged an arrow deep into its eye.

It was a lucky strike. Waylen might have tried ten times to maim the skaler and on nine of those times he might have failed. But his arrowhead had found one of the spongy gaps between the surfaces that formed the jewel of the eye. Squealing, the creature threw back its head, slamming its foe against the ceiling of the cave. Waylen fell with a dead thud, right at Ned's feet. Ned shook in silent revulsion. Oak's end had at least been final and quick. Now here lay Waylen, panting for life, his body broken, his insides mashed.

The skaler was also in trouble. It had pulled right back, banging its head both ways against the wall. The up and down thrash of its colossal tail rocked the whole cave with every brutal thump. It was trying to get out but was stuck near the opening, impeded by a rock its rage had brought down.

And still the darkeyes hadn't moved.

Ned's mind boiled with choices. If he ran while the beast was ailing, he might squeeze past it and escape to the whinneys. But where was the honour in running? Two men were dead (or near enough; Waylen's breathing was reduced to a thread). Their spirits would haunt him for ever if he did not try to win this fight. But whatever he did must be quick and decisive. The skaler had his scent. How long before it came for him again, or more of its kind rallied to its calls?

He risked a look. The beast had ceased to thrash and was in some kind of giddy fall. It was sure to be even more dangerous wounded, but there was no better time to strike. Ned prayed to the Fathers to show him how. They answered with a glint of light. Waylen's knife. It had found a small squint of daylight and bounced it back to Ned's grateful eye. He dropped down and snatched the blade up. It was heavy in his hand and wet with blood. A farming tool with a long curved edge. Waylen had come for a fight, all right. *For friends, now dead*, Ned told himself. He clasped the hilt firmly and stepped out of hiding.

The skaler detected the move right away. It gurgled once, then opened its jaws and filled the cave with a roar that strained every seam of rock.

Ned clamped his ears and was forced to fall back, physically sickened by the weight of air pushing through his body. An ocean of noise raged in his head. It was all he could do to stay level and awake. Panting hard, he spat out some vomit and cut two pieces from the arm of his robe to fold up small and plug into his ears. He fastened one in, surprised he was still alive to do this. Why had the skaler used voice, not fire? Could it be it wanted the darkeyes intact? Why, when the two were mortal enemies? Ned looked at them again. Even now, they were static. Were they dead, he wondered, or locked in a frozen sleep like the animals that wintered when the deep snows came? A spike of frustration rose in him then. And for no other reason than his lack of understanding, he found a loose rock and threw it at the place where the darkeyes were hanging.

There. Let the monsters *wake*.

Even with his ears half stoppered he expected to hear a faint clatter or thump. But the rock just seemed to disappear, as if the creatures had sucked it in. A moment passed, then something extraordinary happened. A wing cracked off the nearest body, turning to dust as it hit the cave floor. A spark of pale pink light appeared and lengthened into a vertical line. Ned's heart thumped against his ribs. His rock had made a hole in what was nothing but a husk. But he'd woken something, of that he was certain. Something very different from the darkeye he'd arrowed in the settlement that time.

Run. There was nothing else for it. He plugged his other ear and jumped out of hiding. 'Kaal!' he screamed, the knife in both hands. He readied himself for a ruthless swing. One good blow before he died. One blow to avenge courageous friends and swell his terrified heart with pride.

But it did not come to that. The skaler was down already, a fire-filled tear rolling out of an eye that bled green around the shaft of Waylen's arrow. It was the most sickening and yet the most wondrous sight Ned had ever seen. He glanced behind him. The light from the darkeye had billowed out into a ghostly spirit. What use was a blade against that? Quickly, Ned sliced a horn off the skaler's head, then threw the knife behind him and ran. Using the dead beast's head as a step, he tumbled along its curving back and out into the daylight.

The whinneys were calm and ready, tethered to a rain-soaked bush. Ned freed the mounts of Oak and Waylen, slapped them and sent them galloping wild. Then he mounted Wind and rode her as her name suggested, away from that eerie cave of death.

On the slope to the river where the three friends had camped, one of Wind's feet found a hole in the ground and brought her down. Ned was thrown headlong into the water. When he turned he saw Wind lying helpless on the bank. Her leg was broken, useless.

'NO!' he screamed, and beat his fists into the water.

And the skies, already heavy with cloud, poured their rain on Ned's fair head, as though his torment was not yet great enough, or his eyes not sufficiently wet with sorrow.

23

Killing a whinney so maimed by injury was a terrible burden, but it had to be done. One strike to Wind's skull and she slept. The rest Ned did with the skaler horn. As the flow of warm air calmed in her nostrils, he blessed her spirit and asked the Fathers to tend her well, until it was his time to cross over into death and he could meet his faithful ride again.

He knelt and stroked her beautiful mane, singing her a song of the open field. And when it became too much for him to bear, he lifted the skaler horn again and thought to plunge it into his heart. How his despondent spirit yearned to feel the point of that worthless prize, but he could not force his hand to do it. If he died here, the tribe would die too. When the skalers discovered the body in the cave, a broken arrow lodged in its eye, their wrath was sure to come down on the Kaal.

Sickened, Ned threw the horn away. He wept for his friends and his beautiful whinney. His life was now worthless, but it must go on. He deserved whatever judgment awaited him, but it would be nothing compared to the murder and ruin the beasts would inflict if they flew against the men. Saving the tribe was all that mattered. It was the only shred of honour he had left.

So he picked himself up and began to run, moving at a pace he thought he could sustain. He ran and ran, through twilight and darkness, finally reaching the outskirts of the settlement just before dawn. Exhausted, he dropped to a shallow in the river and cupped his hands in the cold, clear water, drawing it up to his mouth and face. No skalers. No burning shelters. Still time for the Kaal to escape. He drank again, re-wetting his face, stretching the lids of his weary eyes as if he might wash away the horrors they had witnessed. *Mell*, he whispered to his weary reflection, *I love you, forgive me if they judge me harshly.* On that prayer he made ready to stand, but heard a twig break and held his position. In the half-light he saw the figure of a boy, dipping a vessel into the river.

'Ren?' Ned croaked.

The boy jumped. The vessel clanged against a rock.

'Ren Whitehair?' Ned said, wiping his mouth.

'F-father?' came the reply.

Ned was at him in a matter of strides. He gripped the boy powerfully by the shoulders, squeezing to be sure it was flesh he held and not some lurking spirit. 'Where you bin?' he panted, a rough, bewildered snarl in his voice. He moved his hands to clamp Ren's face.

Ren said, 'Pa, you're hurtin'.'

But Ned held fast, walking Ren backwards as he spoke. 'I bin looking for you, boy, these two days past. Looking. Over the line. For you. Oak and Waylen, they rode out with me. And now they are dead men. Wind gone too. All a'cause of you, boy. All a'cause of *you*.' He pushed Ren over, onto his back. And from a place within the foliage that grew beside the river came a sound that would haunt Ned the rest of his days and steal any sleep still due to him.

Graaarrrk!

He turned swiftly, reaching for a weapon that wasn't there. 'Sweet mercy, what was that?'

Ren rolled to the place where he'd set Pupp down. He clasped the dragon to him, folding its wings. 'Hold yer anger, Pa. Don't fall mad on me. Swear.'

'Heart's fire, boy, what have you found?'

Ren stood up with Pupp in his arms. 'It's young.

226

Ain't no worry to no one.' Slowly, he raised Pupp into the light.

Ned backed away, the juice of his insides rising.

'It were gonna die,' said Ren. 'I was there, watchin', when the mountain waked. I see'd its mother killed by rocks. I ran with it a'cause—'

'Fool,' Ned said, hearing Ren's words but not heeding them. 'Foolish, foolish, foolish boy.' He was laughing and weeping all in one. 'Now we have both brought fire upon the tribe. Now we are dead in more ways than you could dream. Why, boy? What devil made you walk among the beasts?'

'I would save them from the darkeyes,' Ren said boldly.

Ned beat his hands flat to his head. 'There are no *darkeyes*, boy. If you had seen…' But what *had* he seen? What exactly had he freed in the cave? The threat of fire from the skalers was one thing. What now if the tribe was haunted by spirits released from the shell of a demon? 'We must kill it,' he muttered, meaning the pupp. 'Hold it in water. Drown its fire.'

'No,' said Ren, guarding Pupp's head.

'And afterward bury it,' Ned chattered to himself. 'Aye, bury it. Seal it deep in the ground so the beasts will have no scent of it.'

227

'Father, come no closer,' Ren warned. He stepped back, raising the darkeye horn, struggling to keep the little one quiet.

'What's this?' said Ned, the lines around his eyes making plain his bewilderment. He matched steps with Ren as the boy stepped back. 'Would you seek to wound me now?'

Ren jabbed the horn. 'When I hold this, I have the skalers' temper. I can make fire in my hand, like them.'

Ned allowed himself a moment of mirth. 'Boy, I have seen a man vanish in flames. There is nought that you or this fiend you coddle could do to harm me worse.'

'I can,' said Ren, his hand shaking. He could feel Grystina rising again. It was only the thought that this was his father standing before him that was keeping the dragon inside him tethered. 'I am bound to the mother by an oath, deep hidden.'

'Oath?' said Ned. 'You look harsh at your father yet swear a bond to *skalers*?'

On this tender balance of words, Pine Onetooth interrupted them.

'There!' she called from among the trees.

And as Ren chanced to look, his father burst forward and gripped the arm that held the horn. It went spinning out of Ren's grasp. They wrestled a moment, with

Pupp between them. Squealing fearfully, the dragon wiggled and thrust out a wing, slicing Ned's throat just below the ear.

Ned called out in dire pain. He staggered back, stemming the blood with his hand. Ren turned to run, with Pupp in his arms, but walked into the swipe of a wooden club. A second club jarred the back of Ned's head and broke the world up into tiny stars. The last thing he remembered before he hit the ground was the rustle of feet and the voice of Varl Rednose saying in a swagger, 'You done well, girl. This night be yours. Take them. Bag the beast.'

24

Even in these troubled times of darkeyes and skalers, rarely could a man expect to set his gaze on the face of Targen the Old. The leader of the Kaal never left his shelter and would only communicate through his dreyas, the two aged women who attended to his needs and sat beside him during his journeys with the Fathers. It was said that Targen had more years on him than most of the trees in the Whispering Forest. It showed in the many lines of his face, more wrinkled than spiker bark and said to be home to the same kind of nibblers. As Ned was led in and made to kneel, he thought he saw a nibbler scuttle over Targen's rumpled cheek and crawl into the shell of one gnarled brown ear, though it could have been a faint adjustment of expression as the old man framed a look of displeasure.

Ned's head was throbbing, in more than one place. A poultice pasted to the wound at his neck had dried overnight and tugged the edges of the cut together. The pain clawed at the bones of his jaw whenever he tried to open his mouth. One eye was drawing down a veil upon the world. And as if to make his tally of misfortune complete, Varl Rednose had gifted him a swollen ear, the last of the blows to send him into darkness.

Now it was light and the reckoning had begun. Ned hung his head, tormented by the memories clawing at his mind: Ren. The river. The graarking skaler. Oak had judged it right. If only Ned had followed his advice and waited another day for the boy. Now there was tragedy at every turn, and more to come when the skalers arrived. He looked around the shelter. Ren was not there, only Targen and his grisly women, sitting on a pile of animal skins. Between them, in one of the wooden cages used for carrying catches from hunting, was the skaler.

It was lying on its side, twitching now and then. Ned flinched as its claws gripped a bar of the cage and squeezed the wood until it cracked. What strength, he wondered, must an adult have if one so small could splinter a length of wood in its sleep? One of the dreyas bent forward, her grey hair crackling as she stirred the contents of a black pot bedded in the ashes of a fire. Yellow wisps were rising out of it, stinging the air with a grievous scent. The dreya picked up a stick. It was bulbous with rags at the thickest end and heavy with the stains of the potion she was cooking. She stirred the stick into the shallows of the pot and wafted it close to the skaler's snout. The creature's body jerked, then slackened. The dreya sat back with her hands in her lap. She stared at Ned as though his breaths could be numbered by the gaps in her teeth. Ned disliked these women intensely. They were nothing like his Mell, who dressed in simple working robes and warmed his heart with her floating smile. The dreyas never smiled. They wore robes the colour of river mud, sewn with single caarker feathers. In their hair they hung bones that clattered when they spoke. It was said their magicks could turn men to stone. What magicks, Ned wondered, were they planning for him?

'Where is my son?' he asked, needing to support his jaw against the pain.

The second dreya leant close to Targen. She repeated the question as if Ned had spoken a foreign tongue.

Targen opened his toothless mouth. He whispered a faint reply back to the dreya. The words whistled off his breath like arrows.

'He says the tribe is light,' said the dreya. 'He hears death singing among the men. You will speak on this.'

Ned lowered his head. He grimaced and felt the poultice crack. A tear made a pale line down his cheek. 'I rode with Oak Longarm and Waylen Treader. We journeyed by our own consent. We followed the moon in search of the darkeyes, so we might raise them against the skalers. Both these men now lie at peace, slain by a skaler which itself rests dead in the darkeyes' cave, an arrow deep in its blood-drained eye. My soul weeps for brave friends missed, but it will weep a world more if we do not flee the settlement. Do not doubt this: the skalers will come. I say to Targen, the Old, the Wise, do what you will with me, but leave here now and save yourselves.'

The dreya shared these words with Targen and listened, patiently, for his reply.

'He says you must settle the spirits of these men.'

Ned nodded, the tips of his white hair dancing. 'What would he bid me do?'

Targen whispered to the dreya again. She said, 'You will lead the men of the Kaal to the flat rock. You, Whitehair, will carry the skaler.'

A look of surprise set over Ned's face. The flat rock was an old sacrificial stone. It lay some fifty strides wrong

233

of the scorch line and had not been used since Ned was a boy. He shook his head in disbelief. 'You would blood the creature – on skaler ground?'

The dreya consulted Targen again. 'When the skalers come, you will kneel by the stone and return the creature to its kind, unharmed, but a sacrifice will be made.'

'Of what?' said Ned, growing anxious.

The yellow smoke drifted across the shelter. Two bones rattled in the dreya's hair.

'Your son, Whitehair.'

'Ren?' Ned gasped, despite the pain. He looked at Targen. The lines of the old man's face did not lie. 'No,' Ned said. He rose up, struggling to keep his balance. 'If you seek a life, take mine. The boy fell prey to a madness, yes, but I will not give him up in place of this beast.'

'Stay where you stand,' a harsh voice said. Varl Rednose. Again. 'Move and I'll finish what the creature started.'

Ned felt the edge of a sword on his neck.

Two more men swept into the shelter.

'Get him out,' said Varl.

And they dragged Ned away, still in pain, still protesting.

Varl knelt before Targen and bent his head. 'At first

light, it will be done,' he said. Then he nodded at the dreyas and picked up the cage, spitting on the wearling as he carried it into the night.

25

They gagged Ned and tied him to a post overnight, so he might not call Ren or move to flee. Mell was not permitted to see him.

At the break of dawn, Varl woke him with a bucket of watered filth. He gripped Ned's chin with the gag still in place, enjoying the fear he could see in Ned's eyes. 'Were it me,' he said, 'it would be you, not Ren, on that rock this morrow. You are no friend to any Kaal now.' And he spat on Ned's face with even more venom than he'd used for the skaler. Ned heard the creature skrike somewhere and rolled his eyes toward the sound.

'Aye,' said Varl. 'All night the creature called to your boy, and he likeways to it. It's taken him, Ned, chewed on him bad.' He ran a hand down a forearm crowded with scars. 'All this, not flesh no more.

Skaler, he is. Gone wild to the beasts.' He tapped the side of his head. 'Fevered.'

Ned's eyes shrank in disbelief.

Varl nodded. 'Aye, I tell it true. When I blood the boy, I'll be killing the juice o' the skalers in him.' He stepped up close, making Ned recoil from his stinking breath. 'And the spirits of Oak Longarm and Waylen Treader will look upon the green that flows from the cut and smile on my blade and know they are *even*.'

And he punched Ned hard, taking his wind. Ned groaned and wrestled with the ties that bound him. He would have given all the wealth he owned to break free and punch Varl's fat, red nose. But the ties were strong and Ned knew he had lost. A tear ran silver from his grieving eye.

Varl took him again by the chin. 'I am bound by Targen to kill you alike if you choose to make bother. Will you make bother, Ned? Shall I spear you now with this strange black treasure an' save you the long walk to the rock?' He held up the darkeye horn.

In the background, the wearling skriked again.

Ned cursed it silently and said nay with his eyes; nay, he would not make bother. He grunted, wanting to speak.

Varl thought for a moment, then loosened the gag.

Ned coughed away the dry, rank taste in his mouth and seized his chance to breathe cold, sweet air. 'Tell me true. Has Mell seen the arm? Has she seen this change in Ren?'

'Listen hard,' Varl snorted. 'You may hear her weeping – as Oak and Waylen's women weep for them.'

'They rode with me freely,' Ned protested. 'I did no more than—'

Varl stopped him with a brutal slap across the mouth. 'Slight them again and I will cut your tongue till it's twice as skinny as a spiker leaf.'

A bloodied tooth worked free of Ned's gum. He spat it onto the ground and said, 'Will you take me to Ren?'

'You'll see him soon enough.'

'What have you done to him, Varl?'

But Rednose would not say. He pushed the horn into his belt and turned to go.

'Wait!' Ned cried, making several mutts bark.

Varl did him the grace of pausing.

'You swear Ren is bit?'

'Aye,' Varl said. 'Green of arm and babbling like he were born of fire.'

Green of arm? Ned grappled with despair. If this were true and the boy was poisoned, he was as hopeless as Wind with her shattered leg. And so Ned gathered up his grief and said, 'Let it be me.'

Varl half looked back. 'What blether is this?'

'I should be the one to end it,' said Ned. 'Let me be true to the Fathers and the tribe. Let me bear the blade against Ren.'

Varl turned, kicking at a mutt that had drifted too close. 'You ain't got the gristle.'

Ned spat another bead of blood from his mouth. 'You think I want him changed so wrong? It's my right to take back what I seeded. I say to you plain, I stand by the ruling. I will give the skaler back to the beasts and show them the blood of my son, and be done.'

Varl filled his swollen nose with air. He was a pitiless man who cared little for the lives of those around him – but he did understand the need for honour. 'I will think on it,' he said, and walked away.

'Think on it soon!' Ned shouted through his pain. And he glanced up to the sky and whispered, 'Or I tell you true, we are all dead.'

26

They came for Ned shortly. Two to cut him free, two more to drag him to the midst of the settlement where Varl and the rest of the men were waiting. Mell broke free of her guards and threw herself at Ned, pleading with him not to allow them to take Ren to sacrifice. But Ned, by now convinced of his destiny, spoke openly and loud for all to hear. He said that Targen had ruled with wisdom and that he, Ned Whitehair, father of Ren, would settle the spirits of Oak and Waylen by his own strong hand.

'*No-ooo!*' Mell screamed and was dragged away, promising murder on Ned, and worse.

They brought Ren out on an open cart. He was lying on his side, alive but fuddled. His hands were bound in front of him. Ned shuddered when he saw the state of the arm. Varl had spoken true. The boy's flesh was covered in fine green scales that glittered freely in the morning sun. There were bloodstains down his robe, which looked to have come from the blow he'd taken, though Ned suspected they had beaten him too. They had gagged him also, but the cloth was slipping. To his horror, Ned could hear the boy whining, making the sounds the skalers made. A guard punched him hard and tightened the gag. Ned's gaze drifted to the skaler in its cage. That too had been silenced again. It lay squeezed into a corner, a green froth spilling from the angle of its jaw, tail half twined round one of the bars.

Varl strode up, his sword at his side. He nodded at the cage. Ned reluctantly picked it up, holding it well away from his face. The skaler was surprisingly light.

'Aye, be wary it don't bite,' said Varl. He snapped his teeth. The men laughed, but their nerves made the mockery hollow.

Ned liked being taunted as little as anyone, but he saw the wisdom in carrying the cage by its flat wooden base, rather than showing his fingers to the creature. 'I would speak with my son a moment,' he said, a request that Varl straightway denied.

'Your son speaks only with skalers,' he jeered. He

241

mounted his whinney, which tried not to sag beneath his weight. 'Walk,' he ordered, and kicked Ned hard between the shoulders to move him.

By the time they had reached the Whispering Forest, the skaler had woken. It immediately wailed and looked for Ren. Ned had a swift reminder of its strength when its tail whipped the cage, forcing him to drop it. The cage tumbled down a grassy knoll and came to rest in a hopper's hollow. The men roared with laughter to see the beast upside down and kicking. Varl was less impressed. He ordered Ned to retrieve the cage and told another man to find a skin to cover it. For a short while after, the creature was quiet. Then from its dark pen began to come a sound.

Tada, it cried. Over and over. A wail so heavy with woe that it could have drawn the sap from the heart of the trees.

In the cart, Ren stirred. He gestured for water.

Ned looked to Varl for pity.

Varl stroked his beard. 'All right, ungag him. Give the boy water. I need to dampen a tree, anyway. I've enough piss in me to drown a mutt.' The men's

242

laughter shook the forest again. One by one they slid off their whinneys and found places to stand and lift their robes.

Ned used the break to move nearer to Ren. A guard put out a weak hand to stop him, but Ned pushed right on by, saying, 'What harm can there be in speaking to the boy? His time is short. Tend mercifully to him.'

So they hauled Ren into a sitting position, took away his gag and wet his tongue.

Ned said quietly, 'Boy, harken to your father now. You are fevered by skalers, and I must be your remedy.'

Ren's head lolled into his blood-stained chest. '*Garrffred*,' he said in a slur.

Ned looked at the man who was holding Ren. The man shrugged. Like Ned, he could find no meaning for the boy's strange babble. He pulled Ren up by the hair.

'*Galan aug scieth*,' Ren hissed.

The guard backed off, muttering that the boy had been taken by a devil.

'Ren, what are these words?' asked Ned.

'His,' Ren breathed, making soothing sounds that Pupp would understand.

The cage shook in Ned's hands as the skaler grew restless. *Tada*, it wailed. *Tada*. *Tada*.

'His?' said Ned. He thought back on Varl's jibe at the

243

start of the journey. *Your son speaks only with skalers.* Could it be true that Ren had their words? Ned asked directly, 'You speak with the beast?'

'Some,' Ren said, and quickly produced more sounds of dragontongue. The skaler responded with a similar noise and began to jab at the covering skin.

'What does the creature say?' asked Ned.

Ren rolled his eyes. 'It calls me Father, for I am all it has.'

'Let's be on,' barked Varl, reapproaching his whinney.

'And what say you in return?' gulped Ned.

Ren swayed and looked his father in the eye. 'I say I love it – as a father should.'

'Whitehair!' snapped Varl. 'Be done dreaming! I said we are onward. My hand grows eager to slay something.'

One of the men clapped a hand on Ned's shoulder.

'No,' said Ned. He brushed the man off.

Rednose paused and dropped his reins.

By now, Ned's mind was wild with a notion, a notion so strange he could barely believe he would hear himself say it, but say it he did: 'Harken to me. All of you. This errand is false. Targen is wrong. We need Ren alive. He alone can save us.'

Varl's hand moved slowly to the grip of his sword.

'Have a care, Ned. Your words move perilous close to the edge.'

'Take me instead if you must,' Ned shouted, making sure he had the ears of every man. 'But the boy must live. He speaks their tongue.'

Varl drew the blade and held it level at the pulse of Ned's throat. 'He makes an interesting noise, it's true. As will you when I take off your head.'

'I beg you, think on this!' Ned cried. He turned his back on Varl to face more of the men. 'If we can talk to the skalers, we can know their will. We can—'

And that was where his plea was ended, on the pitiless tip of Varl Rednose's sword. It entered Ned's back and pushed out through his front like a milky tongue, bearing nought but the slightest streak of blood.

'No-oo!' Ren screamed, setting Pupp off too.

Ned gasped and dropped the cage. The covering skin fell clear. The skaler flapped and kicked as though all hell was about to rain down.

Varl withdrew his blade, the force of it pulling Ned back against him. 'I told you Ned, no bother,' he whispered.

Ned's mouth bubbled with blood. Despite the pain, he reached back quickly and found Varl's belt. In a moment, the darkeye horn was in his grasp and he had stabbed Varl hard in the groin with it. Varl howled and dropped his sword. Ned fell against the cart and slashed Ren's ties, placing the horn in his son's small hands. 'Whatever you would do, do it now,' he said. And he touched the boy's soft white hair and fell, dead.

By now, the men had recovered their wits and the nearest were beginning to close on Ren. He took the first one down with a burst of fire. The man screamed and fell back, his robe jumping with flames. The others, seeing this, stayed their distance. Some cried out in fear of magicks. Despite his weakened state, Ren tumbled off the cart and staggered to the cage, springing the clasp which held it locked.

'Fly!' he shouted, shaking Pupp out, an act that almost cost him his life. For Varl was injured but certainly not dead. As the drake flapped awkwardly towards the trees, Varl picked up his sword and came there, swinging.

Ren rolled aside as the blade crashed down, its scarred edge splintering the spoke of a wheel. He raised the horn and aimed it true, but Grystina was there in his head and she was saying, *Too many. Flee. Flee!* She was right. Men were coming from all sides now. Some had loaded their bows, awaiting Varl's order to fire.

How? Ren said. *How shall I flee?* But the answer

was with him as soon as he asked. Closing his eyes, he i:maged himself on an open hillside, as light as a wind blowing through tall grass. And instantly he was gone, moving through the barriers of time and space as if he had done no more than push a hand below the surface of a lake.

When he found his wits again he was clear of the forest and out of danger – on his knees in a nearby meadow, within touching distance of the scorch line.

'Pupp,' he whispered, anxious lest the wearling be lost or recaptured. 'Pupp!' he screamed, and immediately started back toward the forest. But Grystina changed his mind again.

Seek them, she said. *Gariffred will hide.*

Them? said Ren.

The Wearle, said she.

Ren looked giddily toward the mountains. In the sky he could see a blue dragon soaring. It looked like the one he'd hidden from three days earlier. Back then, he had needed to avoid its gaze; now he must call the beast to help. So he ran for the scorch line in open sight. Shortly, across it, he found himself stopped by not one, but two huge dragons. The blue one rose and blew fire above his head; the other released a roar so loud that Ren's head went numb and blood ran from his ears. Yet somehow he managed to open his mouth and speak the word Pupp had used repeatedly to him, a word he knew they would understand.

Tada, he said. Before he fell, exhausted, to the ground at their feet.

Part Five

Goyles

27

Although Abrial was the first to see the scales on Ren, Graymere was the one to work out what had happened.

'He's been bitten,' the De:allus murmured.

He nudged Ren onto his back. The boy's arms flopped out in the shape of a cross. There on one hand were the tell-tale teeth marks. Spreading out from a star-like crust at their centre was a perfect set of soft green scales. They had already crossed the wrist and were forking toward the midbone of the arm. Graymere blinked his yellow eyes, but it made no difference to what he was seeing: a Hom infected by the sap of a dragon. In the entire history of dragonkind, nothing like this had ever happened before.

'Look at this,' said Abrial. He was sniffing at something

that had rolled from the boy's hand. 'It's dragon, I think. I'm not sure.'

Graymere looked over. He saw the darkeye horn and thought immediately of the remnant of Rogan, now lodged inside the long scales on his leg. He scanned the piece that Abrial was sniffing at. It looked like a cranial stig. They grew in curving lines behind the ears and were of little use other than to serve a dragon's vanity; the further they extended, the more imposing the dragon was considered to be. Oddly, the stig looked fully formed. That made no sense to Graymere. Stigs of such quality took years to grow. This one was far too small to have come from any adult dragon. 'Is it burned?' he asked.

Abrial ran his nostrils over it. 'I can scent no fire, just fresh Hom blood. How would the Hom get something like this?'

'I don't know,' Graymere said quietly.

But Abrial had a theory. 'Do you think it could have come from the first Wearle?'

By now, Graymere was thinking many things, most of all about that bite. 'Abrial, I have something to tell you. Fanon Grendel believes that Grystina's drake might still be alive.'

Abrial sat up smartly, pricking the fins around his ears. 'How? What does Grendel know?'

Graymere let his gaze run deep beyond the scorch line, his optical triggers panning the hills. 'There's no time to explain. I have to start searching and you need to take this Hom to Prime Galarhade.'

Ren stirred at this point. He gave a terrified start when he saw how close the dragons were and realised the drops of warm fluid on his chest were saliva, dripping from Abrial's jaws. He scrambled away, still low to the ground. In an instant, Abrial brought his tail round and levelled his isoscele at the boy's throat. The dragon growled, but all Ren heard was the rumble in his bones. His head was filled with mush, his hearing shattered by Graymere's roar. He gestured in surrender and tried to speak, but in his fright the words were muddled and mostly Kaal. He saw the horn on the ground and went for it.

With a *whump* that fractured the surrounding soil, Graymere's foot came down on the stig.

Ren jumped again. Out of the balloon that used to be his head, he made sounds that were supposed to say, 'No. Let me have that. I'll show you what I can do with it.' Foolishly, he slapped at Graymere's foot.

The dragon slapped back, catapulting Ren through the air like a fly. The boy landed on his back, groaned and passed out.

'Take him to Galarhade,' Graymere said again.

'But I'm supposed to report to Veng commander Gallen. He—'

'No, not Gallen. Take a route that will keep you clear of the Veng, especially Gazz.'

'Why?'

'Just do it, Abrial.'

'But they'll—'

'Listen to me. The Veng killed Grogan.'

That stopped the blue dead. 'What?'

'They were following Gallen's orders. It happened at the mine. Grogan was sick, poisoned by fhosforent.'

'*Poisoned?* How? Did you send him to Grymric?'

'I wasn't allowed to.'

'By Gallen?'

'By the Elders.'

Abrial took a moment to let this sink in. His teacher. His per. His father's best friend. His crusty old guardian. Dead? 'You...you called him Grogan.'

A ripple ran down Graymere's neck. 'Look into my eyes and tell me the truth: did you cause the quake at Vargos?'

'*No,*' said Abrial. How many times did he have to protest his innocence?

'You weren't attempting to create a physical eruption,

254

just the illusion of one?'

The blue turned his head away. 'Do I look like an Elder?'

No, you don't, thought Graymere, and briefly wanted to run that line of inquiry deeper, but now was not the moment. 'For what it's worth, I believe you were falsely accused. And so does Grendel. Abrial, there's something I need to tell you about myself and Fan—'

'How did he die? How did the Veng kill my per?'

Graymere sighed and shook his head. 'Forget the Veng and any thoughts of vengeance. What matters now is that we find the drake.' *Likewise*, Graymere chided himself, *the situation with Grendel could wait; the blue would know about it soon enough.*

Abrial tightened his claws. 'You truly believe it got out of the mountain?'

Graymere flicked his snout at Ren. 'Only a wearling would speak the word *tada*. Only a wearling could have wounded the boy this gently; you or I would have taken his hand off. The drake is out there somewhere. Dead or alive, he must be found.'

'Where do we begin?'

'I will search; you will return to Skytouch for help.'

'But…if I find the drake, my honour will be restored and—'

'Abrial, you've captured a mutant Hom. That alone will prove your worth to the Elders. Tell the Prime everything I've told you. If you're lucky, he might let you fly the wyng that leads them back here.'

A proud moment that would be. Abrial stood up a little straighter. 'Should I take the stig he was holding?'

Graymere lifted his foot. Though he'd come down on the stig with some force, he'd been careful not to break it. He picked it up and examined it closely, letting its auma feed into his. As he turned it in his claws, a coldness began to crawl through his bones that had nothing to do with the chill in the wind and everything to do with Abrial's earlier question, *Could it have come from the first Wearle?*

'Say nothing of the stig,' he said. And offering no further explanation, he tucked the piece away and spread his wings. He did not have an answer to Abrial's query, except to say that whatever this thing was now, it had definitely been part of a dragon once. It was also tainted with a high concentration of fhosforent.

Just like the remnant he'd taken of Grogan.

28

Abrial took the long way round, coming in on the ocean side of the mountains where the roamers were less likely to be circling and the threat of interference was much reduced. He held Ren clamped between his feet; the boy was alive but barely conscious. At a glance, it looked as if Abrial had been out hunting. It was only when he rounded the peak of Skytouch and glided across the great ice lake that he started to hear the calls.

The blue! Abrial, the blue, is coming! Then the sky began to fill with overlapping roamers and jewelled eyes were glinting on every ledge.

Fearful the Veng would cut across him, Abrial quickened his wingbeats and misjudged the approach to Galarhade's settle – a magnificent depression in the upper half of Skytouch that resembled a dragon's mouth, fully open. (It was the only cave on Erth 'manufactured' by flamework – a construction commissioned by Prime Greffan, leader of the first Wearle.) Abrial pitched forward on landing, swiping his tail to regain stability and smashing several 'fangs' of glistening ice that hung in spines around the lip of the opening. Luckily, he let go of Ren before he put down. The boy hit the cave floor and rolled forward, only to be pinned by the claws of Elder Grynt.

'What in the name of Godith is this?!' It wasn't clear if Grynt was referring to the boy or the intrusion. Abrial decided it was probably both.

'Elder,' he panted, his head low, his wings at half-stretch. 'I bring news from the scorch line.'

'Get out!' roared Grynt. 'Since when did a traitor have the right to invade the Prime dragon's settle and drop...filth like this?!' He scraped Ren to the side of the cave. The boy hit the wall with bone-cracking force. He wailed in pain, but was silenced into a cowering huddle by the threat of Grynt's formidable claws.

'Elder, look at him!' Abrial pleaded. 'He has scales. De:allus Graymere believes he was bitten by a wearling – Grystina's wearling.'

'*What?*'

'Grynt, let him speak,' said a voice from the shadows

258

at the back of the cave. This time it was Prime Galarhade. He sounded weary, unwell.

Grynt powered two columns of smoke from his nostrils. Twisting his face close to Abrial's, he said, 'You have the time it would take me to cut out your primary heart and skewer it onto the peak of this mountain. Trust me, blue, that would not take long.'

Abrial nodded. He didn't doubt Grynt's words; the supreme commander of the Veng had not developed armoured breast scales for nothing. The blue allowed himself a gulp, then told the whole story, leaving out the parts about the stig.

And then the claws did come for Ren. Grynt scooped him up and held him like the carcase of a slain animal.

'Well?' Prime Galarhade croaked.

Grynt's response was to give out a call that instantly brought two roamers to the settle. 'Bring the healer,' he said to one. To the other, 'Summon G'vard and the Veng to Skytouch. Alert me when they are gathered.'

With a whoosh, the roamers were gone.

Grynt turned Ren left and right. 'You say it spoke dragon?'

'From the old tongue,' said Abrial. 'It said "*tada*". A word that only a wear—'

'I know how a young dragon speaks,' snapped Grynt.

Abrial bowed in submission. 'Elder, may I return to the line to aid De:allus Graymere with the search for the drake?'

'You may not,' Grynt said with a quiet growl.

'Speak to it, Grynt,' Prime Galarhade said. Abrial could see him now, hunched in rest, eyes fully closed. He looked on the point of death, which explained why Grynt was here, giving orders.

Elder Grynt shook the boy to bring his head forward. Ren was helpless, a rag in his grasp. 'Pupp...' the boy muttered.

That made no sense to the dragon. 'What are you?' he growled, training his gaze deep into Ren's eye. 'Where is the drake you stole? If you speak our tongue, speak it now, before I crush you like a berry and drink your juice.' He squeezed Ren a little, maybe hoping he would pop out a meaningful word, but all Ren gave was another cry of pain.

'Grynt, we need it alive,' said Galarhade.

Abrial looked again at the Prime. Grynt seemed to be taking no notice of him.

To Abrial's relief, Grymric, the healer, landed in the cave mouth. He threw Abrial a questioning glance – a look soon bettered by the one he gave to Elder Grynt. 'I was gathering herbs nearby when the roamers— What's *that* doing here?'

Grynt dropped the boy at the healer's feet. 'It's been bitten – by a young dragon. The blue fancies it might be the drake, though we have no proof.'

'The drake? *The* drake?' Grymric spluttered.

'Look at it,' the Elder growled.

'Here,' said Abrial, pointing his isoscele at Ren's infected arm.

Grymric mashed the air with his jaws. 'I…this is astonishing. Has De:allus Graymere seen this?'

'He's at the scorch line, looking for the drake,' said Abrial. 'We found—'

'Be quiet,' snapped Grynt. 'Can you make it talk?'

'Talk?' said Grymric.

'It knows some dragontongue,' Abrial said, buffering another dark gaze from the Elder.

Grymric ran his gaze over Ren. 'It would talk better if you didn't break it,' he muttered. 'I have herbs to restore it, but it will take time.'

'We don't have *time*,' Grynt said, as a high-pitched call reached across the cave mouth. The Veng were coming together. This was confirmed a moment later when Gallen swooped into the cave.

His first look also fell on the blue.

'There's been an incident,' barked Grynt, to draw

261

Gallen's attention. 'Call your full wyng. Give half to G'vard and lead the rest yourself.'

'Incident?'

'At the scorch line.'

Gallen glared at Abrial again. 'What position?'

'Show him where you found the boy,' Grynt said.

'Elder, I can lead the wyng my—'

'Show him!' the Elder roared.

And so Abrial i:maged it as best he could.

'Take mappers if you need to,' Grynt told Gallen.

'What are we looking for?' the Veng commander said, his mean eyes thinning as they scrutinised Ren.

'A dragon. A small one. Grystina's drake. Fly as far beyond the line as you need to. Kill anything that resists.'

'No, use restraint,' Prime Galarhade said.

Grymric leant toward the shadows. 'The Prime...?' he queried.

'Unwell,' said Grynt, 'falling in and out of confusion. Your herbs had better be strong, healer. Under the edicts of Ki:meran law, I am leading the Wearle now – and my judgment is sound. Gallen, go.'

The commander was strangely hesitant. 'We are missing five Veng, including Gazz.'

Hearing that name made Abrial start. Hadn't Graymere warned him to avoid Veng Gazz? And now he was *missing*? How? Where?

'Then find them,' said Grynt. 'And be quick about it.'

Gallen gave a sharp nod. With another fierce look at Abrial, he left.

Grynt turned his attention to Abrial and the healer. 'You will speak of this to no other dragon. When the drake is found, this thief will be dealt with.'

'How?' said Abrial.

Grymric cast his gaze to the floor.

Grynt said, 'It will burn before the whole Wearle.'

'But…?'

'But *what*, blue?'

'It ran to us, Elder.'

'And what is that supposed to mean?'

'It means,' Prime Galarhade said in the background, 'that the Hom may have formed a bond with the drake and crossed the line because it needed our help. Would you reward such bravery with burning? We need the Hom alive. It must be given to the De:allus for examination. It may even have links to the first Wearle. Grymric, attend to me now.'

Grymric looked at Elder Grynt, who nodded.

'And the Hom?' Grymric said. 'Shall I try to heal it?'

'No,' said Grynt, narrowing his ridges. 'I know better how to get information from him.' He raised his head and looked squarely at Abrial. 'It pains me to say it, but you have done well.'

Abrial swallowed a ball of smoke. 'May I now aid De:allus Graymere with the search?'

'No. You will return to the line and continue to sweep until this is done.'

Abrial dropped his wings. Elation and disappointment in the space of two sentences.

'This is not a punishment,' Grynt was swift to add. 'With the Veng engaged beyond the line it is more important than ever that you watch for Hom movement. Prove your worth now and your honour will be restored.'

'Really?! I—'

A quick cough from Grymric warned the young dragon not to push it.

'Go swiftly,' Grynt said. 'But before you do, you will carry out one more task.'

Abrial bowed and awaited the command.

'Get this thing out of here and never bring it back.'

'Where shall I take it?'

Grynt looked down at Ren's battered body. 'We need to see into its mind,' he said. 'Take it to Elder Givnay.'

29

Despite the blood spilling out of his groin, Varl Rednose was stout enough of body to continue giving orders to the Kaal. 'Find it,' he growled, meaning Gariffred the drake.

'But the boy?' they jabbered. 'What took 'im, Varl?' Ren had disappeared from their sight with all the speed of a bubble bursting. The men were pale of face, scared. 'And the fire from his hand...'

His hand, they repeated.

Devilry, they murmured.

'I care nowt for the boy,' Rednose thundered. 'Scour the woods. Find the beast. It ain't no flyer yet. Net it tight and bring it back.'

'Fer what?' said Oleg Widefoot, so called because his feet, when together, did not point straight. 'I say it were wrong to kill Ned. Now we are four men dead. Who knows what magicks the boy can call with his father's spirit set loose? I say we go back and seek Targen's wisdom.'

'And what of Oak and Waylen?' Varl snapped, crushing the whispers before they could grow. He pressed a hand to his wound and grimaced. 'Are we not here to rest their spirits? The boy has fled. And he will want to stay fled or eat on this.' He placed a foot on Ned's back and waved his sword under Oleg's chin. Oleg stretched away from its point as if he had smelled a vile brew on the wind. 'The boy has gone to his skaler masters. The only magicks he will bring will come on wings and fire. The young skaler will be our passage, our shield. Now find it, before the treemen do.'

And he swept them, every one, toward the woods as if they were seeds blown loose off a flower.

It took no time to find the drake. Within moments of entering the trees, those leading the search heard a high-pitched squeal and hurried to its source. In a small clearing, untidy with fallen trees and bracken, two treemen were rejoicing a hunting strike. Only one was armed, and he was soon persuaded to drop his spear when he saw he was surrounded by a circle of arrows.

Oleg followed the man's wild gaze. High on the stem of a nearby tree, pinned by a spear through the centre of one wing, was the skaler. It flapped and cried out with a ragged yowl that almost clawed the branches bare.

'Our kill,' the treemen argued.

'Ours now,' said Oleg, showing them a knife. 'Bring it down – and don't lose it.' He jabbed the knife to show he meant business.

The first man spat tamely at him, then sloped toward the tree and climbed it with ease. 'Keep your aim,' Oleg advised the bowmen. The treeman's mossy skin was a perfect blend for the natural browns and greens around him. But he knew better than to risk a flock of arrows in his back. Keeping his face well clear of Gariffred's claws, he pulled out the spear and let the drake fall.

Three Kaal swooped on the creature, netting it tightly as Varl had ordered.

The treeman found a branch and hid from sight, but he was no bother to Oleg now. Kaal and treemen had clashed before, and the outcome for the mossy ones had never been favourable.

Oleg took a bracelet of stones off his wrist and threw it so it landed at the other man's feet. He was scrabbling for it quicker than a snorter could grunt. 'For your trouble,' Oleg said. And to keep the peace. He gestured his men back out of the woods.

They emerged into the light far cheerier of spirit, but their laughter was about to be swiftly arrested. As they filed in straggling lines toward the whinneys, a shadow swept over the ground, accompanied by a scream so unforgiving that no man needed to look into the sky to know what fury was coming.

The drake squealed back, bucking and wriggling despite its injury. The men carrying it panicked and let the net drop. One of them backed up into the trees. He was among the first to die.

Those who chanced to look at the terror would have seen a purple skaler with bright yellow eyes dropping at a steep, sharp angle, fire blazing out of its terrible jaws. It tore a wide line through the edge of the woodland, shooting its flame across the canopy of trees, instantly turning their tops to ash. The men caught under it never stood a chance. Those in the open scattered like peas rolling out of a pot, though any man sluggish of foot was caught by the heat of the creature's next pass as it sprayed the ground in front of the drake. Men and whinneys died where they stood, but Varl Rednose somehow survived both strikes. In the rush to escape he'd been knocked to the ground, his sword fortuitously thrown from his hand. Had he raised it he would have been dead or on fire, and would certainly not have lived to see what happened next.

The skaler was turning, ready to swoop for a third time, when a challenger came out of the sun at its back. It was swift, the new creature. Much smaller than the skaler. Ugly. Vicious. Eyes the colour of dull plums.

Dark.

Making a sound like the jarring of steel against stone, it spat a stream of bile at the skaler's head. The skaler saw it coming and lidded its eyes – but not fast enough. It roared in agony and banked away, flapping its head with so much force that its flight immediately began to falter. It quickly lost height. As it fell, the darkeye came in again, striking for the ears – or more precisely the navigational stigs that gave a dragon its manoeuvrability. Once again, its aim was perfect. The dragon flipped onto its back and dropped like a fading purple star.

It hit the ground with a thump that shook the erth. The darkeye screeched in triumph. It wheeled a full circle, and cast its gaze on the dragon in the net. But as it prepared to drop down and strike, it appeared to be distracted by something in the sky. It turned away rapidly, heading off in the direction from which it had come.

Varl Rednose staggered to his feet.

He picked up his sword and began to chuckle, a small dry sound which turned into a bellow of raucous laughter. 'Men of the Kaal!' he cried. 'We have our VENGEANCE!' And he walked up to the stricken skaler and dared to poke it twice with his sword. It didn't move, but it *was* alive – the flicker in the good eye told him so.

Wiping Ned's blood off his sword, Varl said, 'So, Ned, it seems your spirit has sent us a prize.' And placing his boot on the skaler, he whispered, 'Now you are mine, beast. Now you are mine.'

30

Abrial was not kept long at Elder Givnay's settle. He delivered the boy as instructed and was about to relate the story of his capture when Givnay gave a gentle whine and raised a claw to indicate he should stop. The Elder's gaze fell on Ren's arm. Those lines of scales on pale Hom flesh seemed to be all he needed to see. *Is the drake alive?* he said, pressing the words into Abrial's mind.

'We…believe so,' said Abrial, stuttering slightly. A conversation with the mute was a strange affair. Although it was unnecessary to speak aloud to Givnay, most dragons found it awkward to rely on thoughts alone.

Givnay gave a silent nod. *Leave us*, he said, waving Abrial away. Abrial bowed, glad to be free. Now he could join the search for the drake.

Surprisingly, it hadn't started yet. Despite the urgent orders from Grynt, Gallen was still on the peak of Skytouch, calling his fighting dragons together. The white, G'vard, was with him. As Abrial flew over, he heard them arguing.

The white was growling, 'I don't care how many of your wyng are missing. I'm leaving *now*, whether your *sier pents* fly with me or not.' He exchanged a snarl with one of the two Veng Gallen had assigned to him, a belligerent-looking creature with darker eyes than normal who looked keen to murder anything that might cross its path.

G'vard took off, the Veng at either side, on a course that would take them toward the Hom settlements. Not entirely the wrong direction, but wide of the coordinates Abrial had i:maged.

Abrial sighed at the white's foolhardiness and kept faith with his own instincts, flying for a point between his place of contact with the boy and the large area of woodland close to it. And it was there, at exactly that halfway position, that he encountered the darkeye that had brought down Graymere.

It came at him head on. He could see it was dark and smaller than himself, but he simply assumed it was another dragon. The Wearle dominated the sky.

272

What else could be up here with him?

The rule of grace in situations like this was that the smaller dragon should give way and bank, allowing the larger one to continue unhindered. For once, that right belonged to Abrial. He clearly had the greater wingspan. In fact, he was bigger all round than the other. But it was only as they veered towards a possible collision that he began to question what he was seeing. His optical triggers switched to a narrower focus, recording the creature's ugliness, its high prominence of battle stigs, the strangely dull eye. Even then, he couldn't bring himself to believe it was anything other than a dragon approaching. So he opened his jaws and roared a warning: 'Get out of my way!'

Exactly what the darkeye wanted.

It sucked in and spat its venomous bile, aiming for Abrial's open mouth. Luckily, a favourable gust of wind carried the stream sideways and only droplets hit their target. Abrial retracted his tongue, flooding his mouth with saliva as the bile bit into the soft parts of his palate. He was more stung than hurt, but the pain had done him a precious service: now he was fully alert to the danger.

His battle stigs came up and his scales locked down. Instinct had made him lift and swerve when the bile had hit, a move that granted him enough air space to avoid a slash from the darkeye's claws. They were red at their tips, possibly even poisonous, but nowhere near as thick and sturdy as a dragon's.

He turned fast, but the darkeye turned faster. It flashed underneath him, hacking at his wing with the hard ball of spikes on the end of its tail. Two of the veiny network of bones that held the sheet of the wing together broke, leaving one dangling in the wind. Spurts of bright green blood shot forth. The wing contracted a little, but held. A painful, but not calamitous blow. And Abrial had been lucky. The swipe had caught the rearmost edge. Losing tissue there was a jolt to his vanity, but not a serious injury that would impair flight.

His adversary, however, might not think so.

During his training sessions with per Gorst, Abrial had been warned never to assume an opponent was down until it crashed, unmoving, onto the ground. He put that philosophy to good use now. Rather than turn and re-engage the creature, he deflated his air sacs and allowed himself to drop, as if the strike had been a success. The darkeye gave a victorious aark! and followed him down – a little too leisurely. In an instant, Abrial rolled onto his back and filled the space between them with flame, using rapid blasts of air from his spiracles to flatten the fire into a broad wall of heat.

The creature screamed and dropped through the inferno, most of its lower surfaces on fire. It spat wildly, spraying the air with a red-hot mist of toxic venom. This time, Abrial dodged it with ease. He rolled again, stiffening his isoscele. With one swing, he brought his tail around and slashed through the creature's wing, cutting it off cleanly, close to the body. Black blood burst from the wound. The creature spiralled down, dragging a trail of smoke behind it. Abrial followed it all the way to impact. It hit the erth and sagged, dead, dissolving in a pool of its own foul spit.

Victory. But the blue was shaken. The fight had left him exhausted and hollow. What, exactly, had he killed? More importantly, where had it come from? Clearly, this had to be reported to the Elders, but there was still the drake to think of. And where, he wondered, was De:allus Graymere?

On that thought the wind changed direction and the odour of burned wood pricked his nostrils. Turning his face into the breeze, Abrial scanned the terrain ahead. Right on the edge of his optical range he saw a plume of smoke and the damaged woodland. On the ground near to it, some dots of life were moving round a static purple mound.

It looked like a dragon surrounded by Hom.

He didn't want to believe it was Graymere, but every wingbeat made it more likely. As he came close, the sight of a yellow eye confirmed it. His first impulse as he landed was to kill every Hom in sight. All except one had scattered from the body. A male, plump of build, holding a sword, double-handed, at Graymere's throat.

'One more step and I kill it by my own strong arm!' roared Varl. 'The Kaal will have their vengeance, skaler!'

All of this was mere noise to Abrial.

He started to growl and fill his fire sacs. If the Hom had not been standing by Graymere's head, he would have destroyed it in an instant. But he had seen a faint flicker of life in the dragon and dared not risk extinguishing it.

'If I give word,' Varl barked again, 'my men will fill your young one with arrows. I say stand back, beast!'

Suddenly, Graymere spoke. 'Abrial, is it you?' His voice was thin, as weak as water. To Varl Rednose it would have sounded like a terrified whimper.

'What have they done to you?' Abrial growled. 'Why don't you rise against them?'

'Listen carefully,' Graymere rasped quietly. 'There isn't much time. My limbs are frozen. I can barely speak. Do not come near.'

'But I could crush it or—'

A gargle of pain left Graymere's mouth. In response to Abrial's muted aggression, Varl had roared another warning and leant on Graymere's throat with his sword.

Graymere said in a quiet whine, 'Do as I say. Don't anger the Hom. I must speak while I can. They have the drake.'

On cue, Gariffred let out a pitiful skrike. Abrial swivelled his head and locked his optical triggers onto him. In his keenness to aid Graymere, he had forgotten one of the key rules of battle: keep *all* your senses alert. He should have scented the drake the moment he'd landed.

Varl Rednose rocked his sword. Laughing cruelly, he said, 'Aye, we have it. If you want to hear it squawk again you'll be backin' off and givin' me the life o' this beast!'

Abrial couldn't quite believe what he was seeing. Everything he'd felt that day above Vargos came thudding back.

Grystina.

Her drake.

Alive.

With the *Hom*.

'How did they bring you down?' he muttered, assessing

Gariffred's situation. The young dragon was still netted, a short distance away, snared in an awkward splay of limbs. He'd been abandoned by his captors, but their weapons were firmly trained on him.

'They didn't,' said Graymere. 'It was Gazz.'

'Gazz?'

'You must take an urgent message to Galarhade. The mine must close. The fhosforent is poisonous. Too great an exposure causes a dark mutation in the Veng, possibly other classes too. Once it has taken, it develops rapidly. I saw the changes in Gazz and should have worked it out sooner. It was he who attacked me, I'm sure.'

'Then…I killed him. I flamed a dark creature in the sky just now.'

'Good, but there are going to be others. The Wearle must be put on full alert. Per Grogan was mutating at the point that he died. He took in a large amount of the ore. It occurs to me now that he might have suspected its ill effects and sacrificed himself to warn us of the danger. I have a remnant of his body lodged in my leg scales. It will match the stig the boy was carrying. It's proof of what happened to the first Wearle. Some of those dragons must have mutated and— Raaargh!'

Graymere winced again. Varl Rednose was growing impatient.

So was Abrial. 'If you can move a little, I can burn the Hom with ease.'

'No,' said Graymere. 'Save the drake.'

'I can't. They have their sticks on it.'

'How many?'

'Four.'

'Then pray to Godith their aim is poor. When I tell you to, raise your wings.'

Abrial locked his gaze onto Varl. 'The Hom will kill you if I move. I can read his actions.'

'I know. Let him.'

'But?'

'I'm dying, Abrial. Grymric and his potions can't help me now. You must do as I command and fly the drake to safety. Back away slowly, let the Hom think it's won. Keep your wings down but keep on talking. Did you take the boy to Galarhade?'

'The Prime is ailing,' said Abrial, backing off. 'The boy is with Elder Givnay.'

Varl Rednose roared to his men, 'See this! The beast retreats, beaten!'

Graymere hissed uneasily. 'I don't trust Givnay.'

Abrial blinked in shock. 'But…Elder Givnay is closer to Godith than any of us. How can you question his loyalty to the Wearle?'

'He's been taking too much interest in the mine. More than that, I cannot say. Make a plea to Grynt to keep the boy safe.'

'You think he did come to warn us?'

'I'm sure of it. The drake has been crying out for him. Make ready. Now is the moment. One last thing. Tell Grendel...I'm sorry.'

'Sorry? For what?'

The De:allus sighed. At the corner of his eye, a tear was forming. That immense yellow light was beginning to fade. 'She will know. Be brave. Be strong – for her. I wish I could have known you longer – Gabrial. Raise your wings.'

A few moments of fury, and it was done. The instant Abrial's wings snapped out, the men of the Kaal panicked. Two dropped their weapons and fled. One changed his aim and bounced an arrow off the blue's shoulder. The fourth did loose an arrow at the drake, but his fingers trembled against the string and the dart buried itself in the ground.

Varl Rednose, screaming of death and glory, plunged his sword into Graymere's throat. Graymere's tear had fallen by then, but he had stored enough fire to remind the Hom of what it meant to threaten a dragon. A streak of flame poured out of the gash, igniting Varl from his boots to his beard in a swirling pillar of orange and red.

Abrial roared and ran to Gariffred's side. It was pointless to attempt to free the drake. He merely clamped the net in his jaws, then went back for the remnant in Graymere's leg. By then, the only Hom left on the scene was the burning fat man, Varl Rednose. Abrial moved closer. The Hom was still alive, screaming as he tried to beat down the flames. So Abrial made it easy for him. One stamp put the whole fire out. And with that he took off for Galarhade's settle, wiping the Hom off his foot as he flew.

31

Ren Whitehair ached, in places he never knew a boy could ache. One side of his chest was so weak and tender that the lightest touch made him want to cry out. He dragged his left foot into the light and saw that the ankle was swollen, blue. There was blood on his robe and in his mouth as well where he'd bitten his tongue after hitting the wall of the cave. Blood was also plugging his nose, making breathing difficult and thick. Through his left eye, the world was a dull grey blur; his right was puffy and closed. And his ears, still singing after Graymere's roar, just seemed to be filled with mud. He coughed and felt it keenly in his side, but heard only a muffled expulsion of air. All the same, he had senses enough to know that he was in another cave with another dragon. Every hair on his skin felt the fear as the skaler slanted its head so close that Ren could have put his fingers in its nostrils. He cramped his limbs and tried to make himself small. But it hurt to move and what was the point? Big or small, the beast could rip him apart any time it chose.

'I am Ren, of the Kaal,' he croaked, his tongue pressing painfully against his teeth. The sounds, of course, meant nothing to Givnay. And without the aid of the darkeye horn (and Grystina therefore lying dormant) Ren could form nothing but the simplest words of dragontongue. He tried again, in Kaal. 'I came in fair heart to warn o' the darkeyes. Never wanted to take the pupp – aagh!'

His head jerked back as though a hand had brutally gripped his chin and pushed him hard against the wall – such was the force of Givnay's mind as it entered Ren's consciousness. Ren had never known a feeling like it. It was as if he'd plunged his head into a river and his ears had failed to keep the water out.

You understand me, don't you, Hom?

The voice blew through him like a sudden gust of wind. Ren tried physically to speak, but could muster no more than a stuttering rasp.

I advise you not to resist me, said Givnay. *You may think you are blessed with the strength of a dragon, but I could claw your puny mind to shreds and remove your disgusting arm with one bite.* He snapped his teeth to emphasise the point.

'I swear, I done no wrong,' Ren said. He turned his face away from the fangs.

You're going to show me what you know, said Givnay, *right from the moment you came to Vargos. If you don't, I'll suck it out of you. Believe me, Hom, that would not be pleasant.*

A vision of the scorch line filled Ren's mind.

Cross it, said Givnay. *Show me how you fooled that idiot sweeper.*

He widened the i:mage to bring in the mountains. Ren wept a little to see them. At a basic level, the mountains were what this fight was about. Slowly, he relaxed into his memories. The skies across the i:mage darkened to evening and he saw himself fit and well again, a young boy driven by the thrill of adventure, changing robes, smelling of dung, hiding flat to the ground from skalers.

Givnay snorted in contempt. *Continue.*

Ren showed him everything he could remember, his entry into Vargos, his rescue of the drake, his strange encounter with Grystina. All of it had Givnay bristling. Then Ren showed him the scene on the hill, and how he'd tried to release the drake, only to see it attacked by a dragon with a broken fang. Givnay looked at that memory twice. Only then did he break the connection.

All the pain of Ren's injuries immediately rushed back, squeezing another groan from his lips. His head felt like a scrubbed-out pot. Snatching for breath, he said, 'The pupp were barely born. What's it ever done? Why would your kind want to kill it?'

He swung his head up. The veil across his left eye cleared momentarily and he saw Givnay sitting there, deep in thought, grating one set of claws against the other. It was hard to determine the dragon's size, for the soft grey twists of his long, lean body were blending partially into the rocks. Only the light from his pale green eyes gave any form to his head and neck. Ren panned his gaze further around the cave. Apart from the bones of some unlucky animals, the place was bare – except for an item balanced on an isolated pillar of rock not far from Ren's right shoulder.

At first, he thought it was just a large stone. But after straining a little he saw it was shaped like a cluster of berries. It was dark, the same shade as the horn he'd taken from his father's bed. Perhaps if he could touch it, Grystina would rise and the fire would come? Then he might speak more freely to this other.

He sat up and shuffled sideways.

In a glint the dragon turned, claws extended.

Ren pointed at the 'rock', which was now just above the height of his head. 'I would hold it,' he said, and reached out for it.

Givnay immediately bared his fangs. Ren, fearing a strike was coming, somehow found the strength to duck. *Crack!* The dragon's claws struck a point on the wall where a moment ago Ren's head had rested. They hit with such force Ren heard the tips break. Givnay gave a strangely smothered squeal. He pulled back, holding an arm to his breast. Instinctively, he whipped his tail around and lashed at Ren with a swipe that would have removed the boy's head had the stone pillar not stood in the way. The pillar shuddered. The strange object rolled off. It landed with a thump on the floor of the cave. Givnay hissed, inviting Ren to go for it. Ren knew he would have no chance. One lunge and he'd be joining those animal bones. He lifted his hands in surrender, shaking his head and saying, 'You take it.' For that was why he believed he'd been attacked, because the thing (it looked like a *heart* close up) was some sort of sacred relic.

Whether he was right or wrong, he was spared by the arrival of two other dragons – the green kind, almost identical in size. There was an urgent look in their amber eyes. They spoke rapidly to Givnay (who had swiftly extinguished his temper) and one of them gestured at Ren. Ren's ears were still clotted with blood, but he didn't need to hear a word of dragontongue to read the message the green dragons were conveying.

The colony was under *attack*.

Givnay sucked in through every pore. Still nursing his shattered claws, he glanced at the sky and then at Ren. The interruption had clearly irritated him. All the same, he gave another stifled grunt and before Ren knew it he was in the grip of claws again. The green dragon nearest to him picked him up and flew him at great speed out of the cave. As the cold air hit his battered body, Ren looked at the ice sheets below and half hoped the beast might drop him. He was so giddy with pain that death would be a welcome relief.

But the journey was short and the dragon put him down, gently for once, back at the first cave they'd brought him to. Givnay and the other green followed them in. There were a host of others there now, including the most beautiful skaler Ren had ever seen. She (he guessed it was a female) had intensely blue eyes and golden patterns on her purple face. She was shielding a young one under her wing. Ren was sure it was the infant he'd last seen wrapped in Grystina's tail. He tried to signal to it, but was dragged to one side and put under guard.

A row of dragons was posted at the front of the cave. What they were watching for, Ren didn't know, but before long he heard a rumble of voices and the dragons parted to let another one in. Trapped behind his guard, Ren failed to see it. But the sudden clustering of bodies suggested something important was happening. The large dragon with the silver breast that had done so much to cause Ren's pain gave a sharp roar and the crowd fell back. Then, at last, Ren had a clear view. At the front of the cave was the blue dragon that had carried him into the mountains. Between his feet was Gariffred, the drake, shaking off the strands of a broken net.

Ren filled up with joy. 'Pupp!' he cried. 'Pupp! Pupp!'

Every jewelled eye fell on him. And that allowed the drake a moment of freedom.

Skriking weakly, he hobbled toward Ren, dragging his injured wing along the floor.

Using every scrap of strength he had left, Ren forced his way past his guard. And there, in Galarhade's settle, in sight of the senior dragons of the Wearle, he gathered the wearling into his arms and stroked its spiky head, saying, '*Galan aug scieth. Galan aug scieth.*'

I am you and you are me.

'*Tada*,' the drake said wearily.

And rested his head on Ren's blood-stained shoulder.

32

They were parted quickly, Ren and the drake. Then the arguments began.

'This is an outrage!' Gossana roared. Despite the presence of so many males, the matrial dragon still dominated her surroundings. One blast of her voice had created a tidy space around her. 'Not only do we have this Hom in our midst but you stand by and let it *hold* the drake?'

She rounded on Grynt, whose response was swiftly interrupted by Abrial.

'The Hom helped us save it. They have a bond.'

'*Bond?*' Gossana snarled at him. 'You really are more stupid than I ever thought possible. And still a traitor, despite your lucky…find.'

'No. I believe him.' Grendel came forward. 'I'm

convinced the boy rescued the drake from Vargos. We all heard the words he spoke.'

'Mimicry,' the matrial scoffed. 'Can't you see they're cunning, these creatures?' She turned her head and spat at Ren.

Gariffred immediately skriked his disapproval, which earned him a harsh rebuke from the queen.

'Have a pity. He's injured,' Grendel growled, gathering Gariffred close to her. 'Isn't it clear he feels for the boy?'

Gossana came snout to snout with her. 'You need to dip that pretty purple head into the lake. Hopefully, the ice will clear your mind of any more of these false romantic fantasies.'

But Grendel persisted with her argument, saying, 'When was the last time you taught a wearling a phrase as demanding as *galan aug scieth*? The boy would only hear that from an adult dragon, which gives weight to the theory that—'

'ENOUGH!' barked Grynt, finally taking control. He forced Grendel and Gossana apart. 'There are more important issues at stake than your petty bickering. The drake is returned and we rejoice in that. In time I will hear all sides of the story and will decide what is to be done, especially about the boy. How bad is the drake's injury?'

'A small wing tear,' said Abrial. 'No bones were broken.' He examined his own wing. Already, the severed edge was starting to seal itself for repair.

'Good,' said Grynt. 'Then it will heal quickly and won't be too painful if we have to move them.'

'Move them?' Grendel looked around for an explanation. 'What's happening? Why are we gathered here? And where is Prime Galarhade?'

Grynt replied, 'The Prime is unwell. He is under close supervision in the healer's cave. Myself and Elder Givnay are ruling in his absence.' He glanced briefly at the mute, who had gone back to his poised observational state. Grynt went on, 'You have been brought here for your protection. We have received reports of an unknown enemy, flying near to the—'

'Not unknown,' said Abrial, panting a little, still cooling down after his exertions. 'The enemy are Veng, mutated.'

Veng? Mutated? The words flew around the cave like a chill wind.

Grynt silenced the murmurs with a sharp growl. 'What evidence do you have of this?'

'The D—' Abrial paused and looked hesitantly at Grendel.

'What?' she said. She drew the wearlings to her.

The blue lidded his eyes a little. 'De:allus Graymere was slain by them.'

'What?' gasped Grendel, echoing the shocked response of others. (Gossana merely sniffed and made circles of smoke.) 'Graymere? No. Say it's not so?'

'It is so,' Abrial said gently. And now he understood (or thought he understood) why Graymere had wanted Grendel's forgiveness. She was in her laying cycle. They must have...courted. The thought that Grendel might have been in love with another dragon tugged at Abrial's second heart. But how much worse must it have been for Graymere, knowing he would never see her again?

Even Elder Grynt looked disturbed by the news. 'I asked you for evidence,' he said very quietly. 'Did Graymere find something?'

Abrial nodded. 'Veng Gazz was changed by fhosforent.'

'Changed? To what?' Gossana shortened her snout.

'Into a kind of...*goyle*,' said Abrial, finding a word from the old tongue. 'They are smaller than us, dark of colour. They have no fire, but their spit can burn through a layer of scales.'

'I believe it,' Grendel muttered, her eyes still wide with shock. 'Gazz was stealing fhosforent from the mine. Graymere knew but didn't— He was concerned about the effects the fhosforent was having. He— Oh,

Graymere.' She sank into a huddle. Gayl, the female wearling, whimpered and licked her guardian's snout.

'It was Gazz who attacked him,' Abrial said.

'You saw this?' Grynt asked solemnly.

'De:allus Graymere told me so. I only found him after I'd taken Gazz down.'

'*You* killed a *Veng*?' Gossana hadn't lost the sneer in her voice. She flipped her tail in further disbelief and caught Gariffred a glancing blow across his snout. The wearling squealed in complaint and nipped her. Gossana, her red eyes blazing, turned on him with every fang showing.

'Stop that!' screamed Grendel, on the point of blowing fire. 'Anyone would think you wanted him dead!'

'It's a nuisance. Keep it under control!'

'BE QUIET!' Grynt thundered again. 'I would remind you both of the seriousness of this situation. We are threatened by a dangerous, unfamiliar opponent that has killed a highly-respected dragon. Your trivial squabbling is an insult to his memory. Any more of it and I'll throw you both onto the mountainside without so much as a smoke ring to protect you. Now, you were saying?'

Abrial jumped to attention.

'Speak, blue! You said you killed Gazz?'

Abrial nodded. 'He engaged me in combat, without provocation. I had no choice. Elder, I must show you something.' He brought forth the piece of darkeye that Ren had been carrying.

'A burned stig?' Gossana's words were still laced with scorn. 'Is that all you left of Gazz after your heroic conquest?'

'This didn't come from Gazz, and it's not burned,' said Abrial. 'It was in the boy's hand when he came to us. De:allus Graymere believed it might have come from a previous goyle – one mutated in the first Wearle.' He gave it to Grynt. 'Feel it, Elder.'

Grynt closed his claws around it for a moment, then passed it on to Elder Givnay.

'Now compare it to this,' said Abrial, handing Grynt the wing bone from Grogan.

'This is newer,' said Grynt, 'but its auma is similar.'

'It came from per…Rogan,' Abrial said.

By now this dialogue was causing a considerable stir among the roamers. In addition to Abrial's use of 'goyle', a more chilling word was again being whispered: *Tywyll*. A reference to the fabled aumaless dragon, supposedly a fallen wearling of Godith. A black dragon that carried no fire and whose eyes reflected no light.

The atmosphere in the cave had suddenly become highly charged with fear.

'Look at the boy,' Grendel said suddenly.

Ren was stretching his scaled arm, appealing to Givnay to give him the stig. Givnay was rolling it in his claws and showing no sign of granting the request.

'Elder, let him hold it,' Grendel said.

'What? And kill us all?' Gossana said sharply, saliva dripping like slime off her jaw. She flapped a wingtip at Grynt. 'How do we know that the boy is not in league with these "mutants"? How do we know he won't call them to the cave?'

'If the boy was our enemy,' Abrial argued, 'why would he befriend the drake? The drake respects him. It called him "father". You heard him as well as any of us.'

Gossana blew a line of smoke his way. 'A young dragon will imprint on anything that shows it kindness, you idiot. A falling leaf could lead this wearling astray. Befriending him would make him easier to capture. Have you considered *that*?' She looked at Grynt again. 'How can we be sure that the stig is not a keepsake; a trophy?'

The Elder agreed. 'You,' he said, to one of the roamers. 'Take the boy to a high ledge on Skytouch. Make sure it's one he can't escape from.'

Abrial almost reared in shock. 'But if the goyles come, they'll kill him.'

'Or not,' said Grynt. 'If he's in their command. Until we're certain, he'll be treated as a prisoner.'

'No. You can't—'

'I AM YOUR ELDER!' Grynt roared, a flare of purple around his jaws. 'It is not for you to challenge my ruling. Your rescue of the drake has won you great favour. It will be reported to the Prime when he is well enough to listen. But if he should die, your future is with me. You would do well to remember that.'

Abrial bowed and fell back. He glanced up at Grendel. She looked as frustrated by this ruling as he did.

'Take him,' said Grynt.

The roamer came forward. And while Grendel calmed Gariffred as best she could, with one scoop Ren was lifted and gone.

A not-too-distant cry from outside turned every dragon's gaze to the sky.

'What's happening?' Grynt asked.

'Flames over Vargos,' came the reply.

The battle was coming closer.

'I demand to be released from this cave,' said Gossana, her strutting arrogance oozing forth again. 'I cannot be around frightened wearlings – their scent will draw the mutants to us.'

'How can you say such a thing?' said Grendel.

'This is war,' Gossana snarled. 'Something an innocent like you would know nothing about. If the creatures come, we're trapped in here. I am a queen-elect. I must be protected above all others. What good is a Wearle without eggs?'

'What good is it without Grystina's wearlings?'

'Faah!' Gossana brushed her aside. 'Grynt, if you've got any sense you'll abandon the drake or use it as bait to lure one of the creatures into a trap.'

'Bait?!' roared Grendel.

'It's a liability,' Gossana hissed back.

So much bitterness. Even though he wasn't involved in the spat, Abrial's claws were scratching grooves in the rock beneath his feet. He agreed with Grendel: how could a queen dragon say such things? How could she sacrifice a *drake* to the goyles?! He was amazed that Grynt had let the argument progress, or that he should choose such a stressful moment to turn away and commingle with Elder Givnay. And what was *Givnay* doing to soothe the tension? The spiritual leader of the Wearle had been quieter than usual during these proceedings. For some strange reason, he seemed to be taking a keen interest in the dribbles of saliva on

Gossana's jaw, pointing them out to Grynt.

Grynt said quietly, 'You're certain?'

Givnay gave a solemn nod.

'Clear a path,' Grynt barked at the roamer guard. 'Elder Givnay is leaving.'

'About time,' said Gossana, preparing to follow Givnay out.

'Not you,' said Grynt, blocking her flight. 'You're staying with me.' He nodded at the wet streak on her jaw. 'You're ailing, Matrial.'

Gossana fuddled her head. 'It's nothing. A broken fang. What of it? Now let me out of this cave. I'll take my chances alone with these goyles.'

'You may wish to by the time we're done,' said Grynt.

'*What?*'

'You were seen attacking the drake, when the boy tried to free him outside of Vargos. A dark green dragon with a broken fang in the upper left jaw.'

Every stig on Gossana's head shook with indignation. Both eyes glowed fully red. 'Are you insane? I searched faithfully for the drake as we all did that day. What dragon dares slight my name?'

'No dragon,' Grynt said. 'It was in the boy's mind. Elder Givnay saw it clearly while interrogating him.'

'The BOY?! You believe a HOM over me?'

'I do,' said Grynt. Without warning, he brought his tail around and struck Gossana on a joint of her neck where the nerves of the brain were sited.

The queen staggered and fell with a thump.

'Hhh! Is she dead?' gulped Grendel.

'No,' said Grynt. 'But she'll wish she was when she wakes.' He turned to the roamers. 'Leave, all of you. Post a chain of guards on Skytouch, but don't draw attention to the cave. If the goyles come, fight them in the open.'

He flicked his head and the roamers departed on a clatter of wings.

Turning finally to Abrial, Grynt said, 'Not many moons ago, you wished to be a guardian. Will you be one now?'

'I—?' Abrial gaped wide-eyed at Grendel. 'Yes,' he said, raising his jaw. 'In honour of De:allus Graymere, I pledge myself to Grendel and these young.'

He saw Grendel gulp. She gave a proud nod to say she would accept him.

'Hide them apart, low down,' said Grynt. 'Smear them with any dung that isn't dragon.' Noting Abrial's look of confusion he added, 'It's how the boy got past you at the scorch line. If it worked for him, it might also fool a goyle. When this is done, retrieve the boy and bring him here to me, unharmed.'

Abrial nodded, eager to move. He ushered Grendel and the wearlings to him.

'One last thing.' Grynt waited till he had the blue's gaze once more. 'I said earlier today that you had done well. I say it again now. You have been of great service to the Wearle and your worth is proven beyond all measure. In the eyes of Godith and by the power of the Elders, I call you Gabrial. Your honour is restored.'

'Th-thank you,' said Gabrial, feeling Grendel's isoscele wrapping gently round his.

'Thank me by caring for them,' said Grynt. 'Now go.'

33

When he was a lad of seven winters, Ren had sat astride a whinney with his father and they had ridden to the highest point of the grasslands, where Ned had reined the whinney to a halt, turned them around and pointed to the tallest mountain in the land, the one the Kaal called Longfinger. Thin clouds were hiding Longfinger's peak, but they were running fast across the wide blue sky and before long the tip of the mountain was revealed. Ren, in his joy, had asked his father, 'Have yer climbed it, Pa?' Laughing, Ned had tousled his son's white hair and clamped the boy in his strong, lean arms. 'No man nor beast will tame Longfinger,' he'd said.

But that was before the skalers had come.

The roamer had put Ren down on a ledge, twice as long again as it was deep. No green thing grew there; no flake of snow clung. His only companions were the biting cold and the cushion of a sheer wall of rock at his back. He lay, depleted, in a broken heap, listening to the frequent calls of the dragons, his nose pricking as their pungent bursts of fire were borne across the sky on the shuffling wind. They were fighting, fighting the evil darkeyes, though how the sides were numbered Ren could not tell. Now and then a dragon swept overhead, whupping the air with its sturdy wings. But the battles were mostly distant, nearer to the sleeping mountain than this.

A silhouette against the sun was all Ren saw when he finally encouraged his eyes to blink open. After a time, he supported his chest and dragged himself into a sitting position. The ledge looked over the great ice lake, down the arm of the slow-moving glacier, onward to the boundless, misty sea. Barely days ago, Ren would have thought this a prayer answered: Longfinger tamed and the world spread out in its glory below. But oh, what a price he had paid to be here. Now he was nothing, a hopeless wreck at the mercy of skalers, and no brave father to lean upon.

Shielding his face, he looked across the sky. The sun was still high enough to warm the mountains, but the wind was concealing a spiteful edge. A torn robe was poor defence against it. No matter how Ren tried to wrap the cloth around him, one patch of skin always seemed to burn cold. Worse, each time he sucked for air it felt as if his chest had been cut in half. Out of nothing, he remembered a story from that ride with his father when he was seven. A tale about an invisible giant who lived in a crack on the peak of Longfinger. The giant did not like the Kaal on his mountain and would squeeze a man's chest the higher he climbed until the man could breathe no more and he fell.

Ren thought he could feel the squeeze right now, but the giant that came to land on his ledge was anything but invisible. He turned his face away as a rush of cold air announced the arrival of a dragon. Not the green one that had dropped him here, but the grey patterned scales of Elder Givnay.

Givnay folded his wings down slowly. He peered over the valley as if to check that no other dragon could see him. There was one in the sky some wingbeats away, but it was following a screaming fireball to ground and showing no interest in Ren or his visitor.

Wake, said the mute, invading Ren's mind for the second time that day.

Ren jerked and gripped the rock at his back.

'What do you want, skaler?' He had little love left for the beasts by now. All the glory he'd associated with the word 'dragon' was smeared in his blood on a cave wall somewhere.

Givnay looked around him again. *Show me what you can do with this.*

Something clattered across the ledge. It was the horn Ren had taken from his father's shelter. He studied it hard, wanting to have it, but the memory of the stand-off in Givnay's cave, when that strange stone heart had fallen between them, stayed his hand. Unless he'd been much mistaken, Givnay had wanted to kill him then. He shook his head.

Pick it up, growled the dragon.

'No,' said Ren.

Givnay's eye ridges narrowed. He switched his gaze to a portion of the ledge on the far side of Ren. Moments later, a crack appeared. It ran along the join between the ledge and the rock face and splintered into several thin black roots. The ledge creaked like an old man's knee. Ren scrabbled sideways in terror. 'You're too heavy! Stone's breakin'! Fly!' he shouted.

The ledge groaned. A small piece crumbled away.

What powers did the Astrian give you? snarled Givnay.

Ren shook his head in confusion. He looked frantically

left and right to see where the next crack might appear.

The queen, Grystina. She had the gift of transference. I waited years to take my revenge on her line. And now I find she lives on – in you: galan aug scieth. Reveal her to me! Pick up the stig!

The rock sang again. Another crack weakened the ledge some more, rolling the stig near to Ren's right hand. 'Let me be. I done no harm to you.'

You have, and you know too much, said Givnay, a dark light entering his pale green eyes. *Grystina's father crushed my neck. So I crushed hers while she lay in the mountain. And I would have rid the Wearle of her drake as well, had it not been for your interference.*

'Drake?' said Ren.

Givnay gave a snort of contempt. *This planet has some interesting treasures. The much-maligned mineral, fhosforent, for one. If the Veng had used it wisely they would have discovered that their dark mutation can be controlled. Allow me to demonstrate.*

And there on the ledge, in the plain light of day, one of Givnay's eyes turned red and his grey scales darkened to a deep shade of green. He growled in his curiously stunted way and opened his mouth. In the upper left quarter was a broken fang.

'You!' gasped Ren. 'It were *you* that went for Pupp!'

306

Call Grystina. Now! snapped Givnay. *I want to see her die in your eyes. Call her! Or I will rip out your—*

Whatever Givnay was about to say was cut short by a shadow spreading over the rocks.

'Darkeye!' Ren cried, a fraction too late.

From nowhere, one had risen at Givnay's back. In a blink it had clamped itself onto his shoulders and plunged its fangs into the curve of his neck.

Givnay squealed and threw his head sideways, pounding it so hard against the mountain he almost shook Ren off the ledge. He twisted and managed to spread one wing, but that was the full extent of his resistance. The creature had targeted the vulnerable point where nerves and directional tendons clustered, rendering the Elder dazed and unstable. He rocked dangerously towards the drop. The darkeye raised its head, spitting out scales and blood-green flesh. It had suffered some serious injuries itself. One leg was nothing but an oozing stump and a burn mark had seared the length of its belly. Even so, there was fight left in it. It opened its jaws to take a second bite and must have believed that victory was assured.

But it had not reckoned on Ren.

The boy whistled.

The darkeye paused. It swivelled its gruesome head

and saw a damaged Hom, struggling to stand, holding a stig in its shaking fist.

Ren opened his mouth as wide as he could, hoping the creature would mimic him.

It did.

'Bite on this,' Ren whispered. And he tightened his fingers around the stig and felt Grystina's auma rising. Fire poured into the darkeye's throat. A burst so strong it passed along its gut before exploding out of the tail in a spray of sizzling, acidic pulp. The dull eyes rolled. The claws loosened their grip. The creature slumped sideways, dragging Givnay with it. Both rolled over the edge.

But as Givnay fell, he scored a final triumph. One point of his isoscele hooked onto the ledge, cracking it down a heartline, front to back. The ground beneath Ren's feet gave way. Instantly, he dropped through the gap, skinning his arm against the newly-sheared rock. The pain opened his hand and the stig worked free. Without it he was helpless – no dragon to call upon.

His one hope of escape had gone.

The drop was prolonged, and Longfinger was kind. Its ragged grey slopes made no attempt to break Ren's fall. And so he had time to make his peace with the Fathers. He thought of Mell and Ned and Wind (and Pine Onetooth, strangely, flashed through his mind). But most of all he thought about Pupp. And lastly, he spoke to Grystina. 'Forgive me,' he whispered as the air whistled by.

He closed his eyes, and then it came – the thump that should have brought eternal darkness but instead brought a sweeping whoosh of air. The ice flew past in a blur of white, followed by the upward slant of the mountains. Ren blinked as cold air rippled his face. He was alive and the world was slowing down. Alive and flying again – caught by the claws of a dragon.

Only when Gabrial set him down did Ren Whitehair know the dragon that had saved him. By then, Gariffred was on Ren's chest, licking his wounds in a noisy confusion of joy and distress. Before long, Gayl had joined in too, under the watchful eye of Grendel.

Ren groaned and laid himself out. He looked up at Gabrial and managed a smile.

The blue adjusted his optical triggers and seemed to understand that this movement of the mouth was a gesture of friendship. He bowed his head. 'My name is Gabrial,' he said. 'For all you have done, I pledge you my life.'

The words were too fast for Ren to understand, but he reached out a hand and let it rest on the claws that had saved him. '*Galan aug scieth*,' he whispered.

Gabrial looked at Grendel, who said, 'In memory of the Astrian queen, Grystina, I call you into the Wearle.' And she lowered her head and ran smoke across Ren, saying in return, '*Galan aug scieth.*'

Epilogue

In total, not counting Givnay and Graymere, sixteen dragons were lost in the fighting over Mount Vargos. Only five were goyles, all of them Veng. Gallen, the Veng commander, returned with a break in his isoscele and several melts at the joint of one wing.

G'vard, the white dragon, did not survive. Shortly after setting off to search for Gariffred, the Veng that had snarled at G'vard on Skytouch mutated in mid-flight. They were approaching the Hom settlement when it happened. A savage battle had ensued. G'vard had fought bravely, wounding the goyle but succumbing to its bile in much the same manner that Graymere had. The white had fallen on one of the Kaal shelters, killing two women and one old man. As he dropped, he sprayed his fire in such a frenzy that nearby roofs of straw caught fire and passed their sparks on the wind to others. Before long, the whole Kaal settlement was burning. The second, unaffected Veng, after some confusion, had turned on the goyle and managed to kill it. It had then swooped on the settlement to flame G'vard and put him out of his misery.

It was a sorry tale made worse by the fact that G'vard had ignored the i:maged coordinates in favour of following his personal conviction that the Hom were hiding the drake. There was no suggestion that fhosforent poisoning was to blame for his behaviour. His loss of shading prior to these events had been noticed by dragons other than Grendel, but despite their argument in Grymric's cave, Grendel identified grief as the cause of the white's distress. The healer supported this, and G'vard was duly honoured in the glory of Godith.

Givnay was left to rot where he lay. At the inquiry held by Grynt, the first roamer to attend the body explained that he could not identify it to begin with. Its colouring resembled the matrial, Gossana, but its features were somehow different, he said. Givnay was still clinging to life at that point, but as his fire tear ebbed away the roamer was shocked to see the green scales turning to grey. He was even more disturbed to realise the stricken dragon was Elder Givnay.

When Gabrial was called to give his evidence, he was asked, first of all, why he had deserted Grendel and the wearlings. The blue confessed he had seen what appeared to be a wounded goyle drifting toward the peak of Skytouch. Fearing it would attack Ren, he had flown to intercept. On his approach he had witnessed the final moments of the drama and seen a dark green dragon fall from the ledge. He could not say if it was Givnay or not – but the next witness could.

In what would become an extraordinary twist to the chronicles of dragon lore, a Hom was called before Elder Grynt. Using Gariffred, the drake, to help him channel Grystina's auma, Ren was able to make himself understood. He positively identified Givnay and gave a patchy account of the Elder's motives. All of it confirmed the appalling truth. The mute, with his extraordinary powers of physical i:maging, had started the rock fall that had killed Grystina.

A disturbing revelation, and a terrible blow to the Wearle. Grynt acted quickly to remedy it. Gossana, who had stood accused of Givnay's crimes, was freed and allowed to redeem her honour in any way she saw fit. She seared Givnay's scales to the soft flesh beneath, then turned bitterly to Grynt and said, 'Let anything that finds him chew on him now.' Grynt, in his unopposed role of leader of the Wearle, had agreed.

That same day, Prime Galarhade died of natural causes. He was two hundred and thirty-nine Ki:meran turns old. He had been a companion to four great queens and lived through two ancestral wars. He had witnessed the birth of stars. He saw no part of the fighting with the goyles and shed his fire tear in peace, asleep in Grymric's healing cave.

At his burning, Grynt addressed the Wearle, saying:

'We gather today to commit the auma of this great Elder to shelter under the wings of Godith. Despite the tragedies this Wearle has suffered, he would be proud of what we have achieved. He led us here so we might determine what became of the first Wearle. This battle has given us an answer. We know the first colony mined the fhosforent, doubtless unaware of its harmful effects. Overuse of the ore or prolonged exposure to a concentrated seam causes a dangerous, regressive mutation. It is unclear what triggers the decisive transformation, but when it happens, the change is rapid. For this reason, and because the Veng were primarily affected, commander Gallen has surrendered himself into quarantine until his blood can be cleansed or otherwise investigated. All surviving Veng will also be tested. The mine is now closed, the caches of fhosforent destroyed. The time of these goyles is over.

'Some of you, I know, have been deeply unnerved by what you have seen. I have heard foul whispers that the Tywyll has risen. Such talk will not be tolerated. We go forward with facts, not superstitions. Based on what we have learned, I have reached the conclusion that the first Wearle was drawn into a conflict like ours – and the result was mutual destruction. We have been more fortunate. We have lost many dragons, among them a brave De:allus and the old per, Grogan, whose name we restore and whose memory we honour for his valiant attempt to warn us of these dangers. But our quest to seek Godith in all creation survives. We will continue to explore this planet and its mysteries. The Wearle is everything; the Wearle goes on.'

There were roars of approval all round, the loudest from a family on a nearby hill. Ren was among them, flanked by Gariffred and Gayl. It still hurt Ren to move any limb, but he rested a hand on each of the wearlings and gladly accepted their nuzzles and licks. He was happy for them, truly happy, but he ached to go home and find his mother. The report of fires in the settlement had troubled him. But for now, a return would not be possible. Grynt had given the order that Ren should be kept within the Wearle until he healed. A show of kindness, perhaps, but Ren felt there was some shading in the Elder's words and was already counting the days when he might have to fool the sweepers again and cross the line in the opposite direction.

Nurtured by Grymric's powerful herbs, he was growing stronger with every day. Strangely, now, his scales came and went, but he could feel Grystina's auma always and no longer needed the aid of a stig or Gariffred by his side to call upon her power. Soon he would be ready to run if he needed to – and Gabrial seemed to be aware of it.

As they listened to the last prayers for Galarhade, the blue said, 'Do you hate us, Ren, for the death we have brought on your kind?'

Not hate, thought Ren. Hate was too strong a word. He flicked away a blade of grass. 'I miss my pa.'

'Pa?' said Gabrial. This was a Hom word new to him.

'Tada – father,' Ren translated.

Gabrial nodded. His claws pressed a little tighter to the ground, churning gentle furrows in the erth. 'I lost my father in battle.'

Ren looked up into the great blue eyes.

'He was here with the first Wearle,' Gabrial said.

Far below them, Galarhade's body caught fire. The sudden *whumph* made Gayl cry out in fright. Gariffred sat up as if he'd seen a star fall out of the sky.

'Come,' said Grendel, ushering him to her. She gathered both wearlings under her wings.

Ren picked a small flower, leaving enough of the stalk to twirl in his fingers. 'Dint know about yer pa. I'm sorry.'

The blue let a quiet moment pass. 'He was a mapper,' he said.

'Muh…?' Ren said.

Gabrial pronounced it again, more slowly. 'Map-per.' Ren's grasp of dragontongue was fast improving, though some expressions still bounced around his ears like muddled growls.

'Map-per,' the boy repeated.

'Hrrr,' said the dragon, meaning 'good'.

Ren smiled and looked at the flower in his hands. It had six pink petals and a black centre. It made him think of the pink-coloured crystals that had turned some dragons into goyles. What if Gabrial's father…?

He shuddered, not wanting to go where that thought was taking him.

'Are you cold?' asked Gabrial.

Ren shook his head. 'No.'

Gabrial lifted a foot, flexing his claws to be rid of the dirt. 'We must go, both of us.'

'Where?'

'To Galarhade.'

A small sigh betrayed Ren's thoughts. It was a long walk down the hill from here.

'You would honour the Wearle if you did,' said Gabrial.

Honour. Of course. Ren stood up and threw away the flower. He sighed again as he measured the distance.

Gabrial tilted his head in query.

'Long way,' said Ren. He made walking movements with his fingers.

The dragon's eye ridges narrowed. He tried to move his claws in the same way as Ren's fingers; the Hom had some strange abilities, he thought. He bent his knees, dropping his wings to a comfortable height.

'REALLY?' gasped Ren. They were going to fly?!

'Swiftly, before Grendel burns my ears,' said the blue.

Ren did not need a second invitation. He scrambled up the stairway made by the wing bones and sat astride Gabrial's giant neck. The warmth from the dragon's body was amazing, even if the scales were uncomfortable to sit on. 'Does this hurt?' Ren asked, taking hold of two stigs for balance.

Gabrial snorted and put out his wings.

'Waah!' cried Ren, gasping and laughing as the dragon rose up.

'Ready?' said Gabrial.

Ren tightened his grip. In his best broken dragontongue, he gabbled, 'One day, we will fly to my home and make peace between skalers and the Kaal.'

Gabrial's eye ridges creaked again. Ren's words were like raindrops tossed in a storm. But the beat of the boy's heart told its own story. Gabrial matched it with a positive hrrr!

And they took off into the crisp blue sky.

A boy and a dragon, at peace.

But peace was not on everyone's mind. On the far side of the scorch line, Mell, wife of the tragic Ned Whitehair, was sitting alone by the river, idly making a chain of flowers. Behind her, dying columns of smoke still marked the invasion of the skalers and their war.

So lost in her thoughts was Mell that she did not hear a whinney approaching, until it was blowing its warm breath over her.

She looked up, cupping her eyes against the sun. 'Do I know you?' she said, even though the rider was a stranger to her.

He smiled, but did not reply at first. His hair was thin and its colour blacker than the nose of a mutt. It fell in curling strands to his shoulders. He was wearing a robe the kind of which Mell had never seen before. Sleek, it was, like the fur of a hopper, but shining here and there like a skaler wing.

Odder still was his ride.

'What kind of whinney would that be?' she asked.

It was white, the whinney, with a flowing mane and a spiralling horn protruding from its forehead. There was a strange and distant light in its eye, a light the colour of an evening sky that would herald sunshine on the dawn.

'I found it so,' said the man. 'I seek shelter, woman. Will you give it?'

'I would, if I had it to give,' said Mell. 'The skalers have burned what was mine, what was Kaal.'

The man reined round and stared at the mountains. 'I have no love for skalers,' he said.

Mell bowed and felt a tingle of joy. She liked this stranger's sureness of heart. 'You have the eyes of someone I knew,' she said. 'A brave man, a farmer, now resting with the Fathers. He went by the name of Waylen Treader. Are you kin to him?'

'I have no kin,' said the man. And now, Mell noticed, his eyes for a moment glowed the colour of those that defined his whinney.

'Nor I,' she said, throwing her flower chain into the river. She fought back a tear as it floated away. 'Our leader, Targen the Old, is dead, along with half our men. My man and my boy are both gone.' She gestured at the mountains so the stranger knew her meaning.

'Then join me,' he said.

'I might,' said Mell, stroking her hair where it fell across her shoulder. 'First, I will need a name to call you.'

The stranger extended his hand to her. 'I have only one name,' he said. 'Tywyll.'

Acknowledgments

I'm going to do this right, for once, and put Jay at the top of the thank you list. Frankly, without her, *The Wearle* wouldn't be half the book it is. Someone once told me there are as many ways of writing a story as there are people out there doing it. Our way is a painstaking collaboration of ideas, something that doesn't stop after the initial idea is mooted, but continues on through chapter after chapter, edit after edit, rewrite after rewrite. I always knew it would be an interesting challenge to write an anthropomorphic saga about a dragon colony, but I wasn't sure this level of fantasy would suit my writing style. It was Jay who insisted it would. But for her dedication and enthusiasm, the project might never have taken flight (sorry). So, reader, if you like the story, praise Jay for her tireless hard work, as I do here.

Another huge enthusiast was Sarah Leonard, my editor. She was new to me at the start of this project and also new to Orchard Books. I have to pause at this point to offer tangential praise to Orchard's publishing director, Megan Larkin. It was Megan who directed me towards Sarah, because their new acquisition was not only a talented up-and-coming editor, but also loved dragons. Sarah's thorough, insightful and passionate comments have helped add an extra dimension to the book and I eagerly look forward to our next Erth encounter. Staying with Orchard for a moment, I also owe a huge debt of gratitude to their recently retired MD, Marlene Johnson, not just for this book, but for all my books with them. Better late than never, eh, Marlene?

And then there is the lovely Bethan Hughes, my 'tame Welsh librarian'. Over the years, many children have asked me how to speak dragontongue. My reply has always been that the nearest human language to it is Welsh – not that Welsh gave rise to dragontongue, you understand, it was clearly the other way round, and both languages have since evolved in slightly separate ways. Even so, you will find a number of places in the text where a word or two of the 'old tongue' has crept in, and I am deeply grateful to Bethan for finding her fire within and translating the text as near as possible to the dragons' intended meaning. Any liberties, mistakes or ambiguities are all attributable to me.

And finally, I want to thank the thousands of children (and adults) who have written to me over the years in praise of *The Last Dragon Chronicles*. You won't find the likes of David or Gadzooks in this book, but I hope you'll discover a whole new set of reasons to renew your passion for dragons. Hrrr!

Glossary

Auma – the lifeforce or spirit of a dragon, derived from an ancient word for 'fire'. When a dragon dies and sheds its fire tear, its auma is believed to return to the creator, Godith.

Bleater – Hom name for a goat (and sometimes a sheep).

Blether – to speak nonsense, as in: 'What blether are you saying now, boy?'

Buzzer – Hom name for a fly.

Caarker – Hom name for a crow. Crows are deeply revered by the Hom and thought to be the most intelligent of birds. Hom women will often wear black crow feathers in their hair, while men might string the claws around their necks to bring them luck in hunting.

Cold flame – under certain atmospheric conditions,

dragons are capable of producing a cool flame (pale blue in colour) that would cause skin burns but not ignite combustible materials such as wood.

Commingle – a 'coming together', usually of minds. All dragons develop the ability to communicate telepathically, i.e. using thought alone. A deeper extension of telepathy is commingling, in which a dragon focuses its awareness to such an extent that it is able to meld with another dragon's consciousness and read or know *all* of that dragon's thoughts. Commingling is invasive and banned by Ki:meran law unless both parties consent. (Courting dragons, for example, might commingle to explore their love for one another.) During colonisation, an elder highly skilled in commingling will meld with a variety of life forms on a planet to determine their level of intelligence or their potential threat to the colony.

De:allus – a highly-intellectual class of dragon whose lives are devoted to understanding the wonders of Godith's universe. De:allus are scientists or problem-solvers, characterised by their bright yellow eyes. It is not known how their eye colour developed, though it's often said (somewhat disparagingly) that their optical triggers have become impaired because the De:allus like to look too long at *small* things.

Domayne – any parcel of land claimed by a dragon;

their home territory. The term can also describe a large region of land mapped out during colonisation.

Drake – a young male dragon (sometimes also called a weardrake). A dragon will usually lose this tag around its second turn.

Dreyas – Hom women, practised in the art of 'magicks'. A sick person might go to a dreya for a healing potion.

Elder – a senior dragon (usually male) whose role is to steer and advise the colony. Three Elders would usually accompany a large Wearle: one to maintain law and order, one to attend to the spiritual needs of the community and one designated as the overall leader or Prime.

Erth – home planet of the Hom.

Eyrie – an ancient word of dragontongue meaning 'high nest'. Now more commonly used to describe a superior cave or settle, such as that of a queen or the Prime dragon.

Faah! – a shocking or vulgar exclamation.

Fanon – a word from the old dragontongue meaning 'a female yet to have young'.

Fhosforent – pink crystalline mineral found in Erth's volcanic rock. In small quantities it improves a dragon's flame by causing a rapid enlargement of the fire sacs, allowing more fire to be produced and delivered.

Fire star – a portal in time and space, called a 'star' because of the flash of light emitted when something passes through it. Among the many abilities dragons possess is the means to manipulate the fabric of the universe to create 'holes' or openings in space, through which they might travel vast distances. To i:mage a fire star requires an enormous amount of mental energy (two or three Elders commingling to produce it), but once an opening is created, space 'remembers' the point. It is then a relatively simple matter for a competent dragon to open and close a fire star at will.

Fire tear – a single tear cried by a dragon at its death, said to contain its auma in the form of a spark. How a fire tear develops is one of the great mysteries of Godith's universe. When the tear is shed, it is drawn below the surface of a planet by the pull of the fire at the planet's core (this is known as the 'calling' or the 'calling of Godith'). The moment the fires combine, the dragon's body will begin to dissolve, leaving no visible remains. As a mark of respect, and because the calling of a dragon can take several days, a dead dragon might first be cremated in the flames of its peers. In extreme circumstances a dragon might die without shedding its tear. In this case its primary heart will turn to stone, along with the rest of its body if it is not burned. To die and not be called to Godith is the worst fate that can befall a dragon.

Flapper – Hom name for a bat.

Flutterfly – Hom name for a butterfly.

Frenhines fawr – 'great queen' in the old dragontongue, an expression of deep respect, usually reserved for a female who has given birth to two or more sets of wearlings.

Glamouring – a rarely-used word which describes a dragon's ability to mesmerise others (usually prey) with a stare.

Goyle – in their early years wearlings were sometimes told a traditional tale about 'Goyle', a dragon that emerged from 'the wrong end of his egg'. Goyle was alleged to be so unsightly that to look upon him would make a dragon shudder so much its scales would drop off. Over the generations it has come to mean anything ugly or grotesque.

Growler – Hom name for a bear.

Guardian – a male companion who protects a matrial and her wearlings (see laying cycle).

Heart(s) – dragons have three hearts, closely linked. The largest, the primary heart, drives the body and is concerned with power and strength; the second, about three fifths the size of the primary heart, controls love and emotional reactions; the third, which is small and just hidden by the second heart, gives a dragon its spirituality.

Hom – an early form of the human race.

Honker – Hom name for a goose.

Hooter – Hom name for an owl.

Hopper – Hom name for a rabbit.

I:mage – the ability to create external structures from mental images. There are two types of i:maging, *physical* and *natural* (see also phasing). A natural i:mage is a floating three-dimensional picture (a kind of hologram) that fades as soon as it outlives its usefulness – a map, for instance, or the memory of an event. Physical i:maging is used to create more permanent objects or to alter the parameters of *existing* matter. It can take a lifetime of dedicated study to reach even a modest level of competence.

Isoscele – the triangular scale at the end of a dragon's tail, primarily for balance but also a useful tool in battle (sometimes called the 'hidden claw') and commonly used to point or gesture.

Kaal – a tribe of humans. The origin of the name is

thought to derive from 'cave' and refers to the Kaal's preferred choice of habitat: any mountainous region near water.

Ki:mera – the homeworld of dragons, created for them by the breath of Godith. Literally meaning 'place of fire and light'.

Laying cycle – the process of giving birth to young. During their lifetime all healthy female dragons will enter at least two laying cycles, and sometimes as many as four. Dragons give birth by the process of parthenogenesis. A female can produce, lay and hatch her eggs without the assistance of a male. It is only after the young are born that the male becomes a vital part of the bloodline. A male that successfully bonds to a female is called her companion, a position he must fight for. As guardian to her young, he also earns the right to call himself 'father'. Only when the female emerges from her nest with her young does she discover who the father will be. The next few months are crucial, for it is during this time that the young dragons *imprint* themselves on the father, and the necessary hormonal and behavioural changes take place which establish them as part of the father's bloodline.

Lytes – scales that sparkle, usually on the more protected parts of the body, under wings, for example. Traditionally, too many lytes were considered to detract from a male dragon's potency. Some have been known to rip lytes off or 'weather' them to make them darker, though opinions are changing.

Mapper – a dragon who maps out territories, especially beyond the boundaries of the domayne. A good mapper can 'record' the layout of a land mass from a variety of heights or directional approaches and reproduce it accurately, in the form of an i:mage, for other dragons to see.

Matrial – an honorific title for a female dragon who has had wearlings.

Mutt – Hom name for a dog.

Myss – (or wearmyss) a young female dragon.

Nibbler – Hom name for any kind of small bug.

Per – an honorific title given to a dragon who mentors a younger dragon or one of lesser status. Older dragons (usually, but not exclusively, males) experienced in the techniques of flying, phasing, i:maging, fighting, mapping, daily grooming and courtship, are expected to pass on their knowledge to their younger counterparts, particularly if the parents are absent for any reason. Pers are also teachers and historians, charged with chronicling the events of the past and keeping traditions alive.

Phasing – the ability to move through time during flight. One of the most potent weapons in a dragon's armoury is the ability to surprise (or escape from) an opponent by briefly 'skipping' time. Under the right conditions a phasing dragon can close (or extend) a gap between itself and another point in space in the *exact* time it would take to think of the movement, thereby appearing to 'jump' the gap. The technique is an advanced and sophisticated form of i:maging, in which the dragon must be able to 'see' itself ahead of time and then 'dissolve' into the dark energy of the universe as if it were no heavier than a breath of wind. Many dragons never master it. Some even die in the process.

Plentyn – a word from the old dragontongue meaning 'child'.

Prime – an elder who is also the supreme leader of a dragon colony.

Pupp – Hom name for a young mutt (dog), but can be used for any young creature.

Queen – female dragon who has hatched wearlings and brought them safely out of the birthing cave.

Roamer – a young dragon who has reached sufficient maturity to be allowed to 'roam' where he or she pleases, within reason. Nearly half of a colonising Wearle will be made up of roamers. Most will be allotted simple duties, such as carrying messages or assisting the elders. Many become scouts, sent to the far edges of the domayne and beyond to report back anything they find to the mappers or the Veng.

Sawfin – fine scales in a ruff shape behind a female dragon's ears.

Scorch line – the line charred on the ground to separate the colony's domayne from the Hom, who must not cross it.

Scratcher – Hom name for a mouse.

Settle – a resting place. In mountain regions a dragon will settle anywhere high. Barring caves (which are reserved for elders or others of high importance) the most sought-after locations are rocky outcrops (where the dragon can proudly display its outline against the sky) or ledges.

Shimmy – Hom name for a fish.

Sier pents – term meaning 'green fish', used in a derogatory way to describe the Veng.

Skaler – Hom name for a dragon.

Skrike – the cry of a young wearling.

Slitherer – Hom name for a snake.

Snorter – Hom name for a pig.

Spiker – Hom word for a pine tree.

Spiracles – breathing holes in a dragon's body, most notably along the sides of the throat. A valve close to each hole aids the intake of oxygen when fire is being formed and helps relieve air pressure during the expulsion of flame. The spiracles are heavily shielded by 'spiracites', small hardened scales that can be closed independently over the holes. If the spiracles become damaged or clogged, a dragon can become severely impaired.

Sweeper – a dragon who patrols the scorch line, checking for incursions or threats.

Tada – a word for 'father', from the old dragontongue.

Transference – the ability to transfer huge amounts of information and even some powers by commingling. A very rare gift, possessed by only a few dragons. Females of the Astrian bloodline are many times more likely to have transference skills, for reasons as yet unknown.

Turn – a Ki:meran year.

Tywyll – a fabled fallen wearling of Godith, a black dragon born without a third heart, whose eyes reflect no light. In the old tongue, Tywyll means 'the darkness'. For all their power, dragons can be superstitious creatures. Nothing troubles their dreams more than the thought of the Tywyll rising.

Vapor – a floating dragon spirit, a 'ghost'.

Veng – a particularly fearsome class of fighting dragon, used as security for a colony. The Veng rarely breed outside their own class. As such, there is minimal genetic variation in their colour (bright green), temperament (aggressive) or physical composition (thin, strong and very agile). The Veng are the one dragon class most other dragons fear.

Wearle – a large community of dragons. A Wearle would number more than a wyng, but anything more than a hundred dragons would be considered a fixed colony. There were twenty-four dragons in the first Wearle to visit Erth, sixty in the second.

Wearling – a young dragon of either gender.

Webber – Hom name for a spider.

Whinney – Hom name for a horse.

Wyng – a small group of dragons with a common purpose (e.g. a fighting wyng).